FILIAL PIETY
AND ITS
DIVINE REWARDS

FILIAL PIETY AND ITS DIVINE REWARDS

The Legend of Dong Yong and Weaving Maiden
with Related Texts

Edited and Translated,
with an Introduction,
by

Wilt L. Idema

Hackett Publishing Company, Inc.
Indianapolis/Cambridge

14 13 12 11 10 09   1 2 3 4 5 6 7

For further information, please address:

Hackett Publishing Company, Inc.
P.O. Box 44937
Indianapolis, Indiana 46244-0937

www.hackettpublishing.com

Cover design by Abigail Coyle
Text design and composition by Carrie Wagner
Printed at Malloy, Inc.

Library of Congress Cataloging-in-Publication Data

Filial piety and its divine rewards : the legend of Dong Yong and Weaving
Maiden with related texts / edited and translated, with introduction, by Wilt
L. Idema.

p. cm.

Includes bibliographical references.

ISBN 978-1-60384-135-1 (pbk.) -- ISBN 978-1-60384-136-8 (cloth)
1. Dong, Yong (Legendary character)--Legends. 2. Zhi Nü (Chinese deity)--
Legends. 3. Filial piety--China--Folklore. I. Idema, W. L. (Wilt L.) II. Title:
Legend of Dong Yong and Weaving Maiden with related texts.
GR335.4.D65F55 2009
398.20951--dc22

2009025798

Dong Yong practiced filial piety, and the Emperor of Heaven ordered one of the immortal maidens to marry him. When the other immortal maidens saw her off, they all urged her: "Make sure to send a letter if down in the world below you find yet another filial son!"

From Feng Menglong (1574–1646), Comp., A Treasury of Laughs (Xiaofu)

(Wang Liqi, 1957, 300)

A Song to the Tune of *Jishengcao*

Seventh Immortal Sister arrived at the old scholartree;
She looked at the earth and then gazed upon heaven:
"Once I leave I'll never be able to see my true love again!
A match so fine really becomes a dry sea, a smashed rock.
This is a case where passion and law are in conflict:
Oh, how I would love to have a torch to burn this *Tale of Dong Yong!*
Oh, how I would love to have a torch to burn this *Tale of Dong Yong!*"

An anonymous song of the Qianlong-Jiaqing period (1736–1820)
preserved in manuscript

(Du, 1957, 25)

CONTENTS

PREFACE

The exploits of Mulan, the legend of the White Snake, the romance of Liang Shanbo and Zhu Yingtai, and the thwarted love of Weaving Maiden and Buffalo Boy continue to fascinate Chinese audiences all over the world. As the embodiment of Chinese people's wisdom, virtue, and pursuit of love, these tales have been told and retold throughout the twentieth century; they have also been performed on the stage, adapted for the screen, and rewritten as dramas for television. They have inspired theme parks and postage stamps, violin concertos, and Western-style operas. In their modern transformations these traditional tales have been hailed as the quintessence of Chinese culture, as instruments for cultural renewal, and as tools of criticism.

The earliest extant premodern versions of these Chinese tales and legends are no less varied and multiform than their modern adaptations. By the time they were recorded, each of these stories had already undergone a centuries-long period of development and change. Depending on the time, region, and genre in which it was created, each version is unique and brings its own perspective and meaning to the story. Moreover, each of these texts reflects the idiosyncrasies and personality of its author (whose name has usually been lost). We could make no greater mistake than to assume that these stories embodied a single, unchanging, essential meaning, even though many modern and contemporary scholars write about these stories as if they did.

Despite the popularity of these tales and legends among modern and contemporary authors and intellectuals, in late-imperial times such tales and legends (with the exception of *Mulan*) were mostly ignored by the scholars and literati of the Ming (1368–1644) and the Qing (1644–1911) dynasties. Nonetheless, these texts flourished in the realm of oral literature and in the many genres of traditional popular literature (*suwenxue*). This series aims to introduce the contemporary English reader to the richness and variety of traditional Chinese popular literature of late-imperial China, and to the wide discrepancies between the different adaptations of each story by translating at least two different premodern adaptations in full. Each of these sets of translations will be preceded by an introduction tracing the historical development of each story up to the beginning of the twentieth century. The translations will be followed by a selection of related materials that will provide the readers with a fuller understanding of the historical development of each story, and help them place the translated text in the development of Chinese popular literature and culture.

ACKNOWLEDGMENTS

First of all, it is my pleasure to express my thanks to the staff of the Harvard-Yenching Library for their help in locating and acquiring primary and secondary materials. The Harvard-Yenching is not only a great library because of its unsurpassed holdings, but also because of the gracious professionalism of its staff.

Secondly I would like to thank my colleague David Wang, for his willingness to coteach with me CL 150, in which we discussed the premodern transformation and modern appropriations of China's most famous legends and folktales. I would also like to thank the Teaching Fellows and students who took part in that class. Each of them stimulated me, directly or indirectly, to improve the translations in this volume and their introduction.

Thirdly I would like to thank the highly professional staff at Hackett Publishing Company for their efficiency in handling all aspects of the production process.

Wilt L. Idema

INTRODUCTION

The foundational virtue of imperial China was filial piety (*xiao*). Other cultures also required children to respect and obey their parents, to take care of their parents in old age, and to provide them with a burial appropriate to the family's status. For the Chinese, however, filial piety included a religious meaning as well, because it required children to maintain the sacrifices to the ancestors in order to ensure the family's continued prosperity. Because of this, the greatest crime against filial piety for a son was a failure to produce descendants.[1]

The duties of filial piety were detailed in philosophical treatises and moral tracts, while concrete models of exemplary and extreme filial piety were provided by biographies of filial sons. One of the most popular primers of the last dynasties was *The Twenty-Four Exemplars of Filial Piety* (*Ershisi xiao*), which in its present form dates from the Yuan dynasty (1260–1368). It provides the potted biographies of twenty-three filial sons and one filial daughter-in-law, each concluded by a four-line summarizing poem. To enhance the book's attraction to young readers, each biography is illustrated by a large picture. Most of these stories are rather dreary, and some are pretty grim,[2] but the story of Dong Yong is a charming fairy tale and reads:

Selling One's Body to Bury One's Father

Dong Yong of the Han was so poor that when his father died he sold his body into servitude and buried him with borrowed money. When he set out to repay his debt through labor, he met a woman while on the road. She wanted to be his wife, and together they arrived at his master's house. The master ordered her to weave three hundred bolts of double-threaded silk, and then they could go back. After only one month she

---

[1] The scholarly literature on filial piety is too extensive to be summarized here. For a recent collection discussing various aspects of filial piety in past and present, see Chan and Tan, 2004.

[2] The modern writer Lu Xun (1881–1936) has described his memories of reading *The Twenty-Four Exemplars of Filial Piety* as a child. See his "The Picture-Book of the Twenty-Four Acts of Filial Piety" in Lu Hsün, 1976, 26–35.

had completed the task. When on the way back home they arrived at the
spot where they had met in the shade of a scholartree,[3] she said good-
bye to Yong and disappeared.

> To bury his father he needed to borrow money;
> Out on the road he ran into an immortal beauty.
> Weaving silk she paid off his debt to his master:
> His filial piety managed to move the sky above![4]

Many of the stories of *The Twenty-Four Exemplars of Filial Piety* were adapted
for the stage and retold in narrative ballads in late-imperial China, but none
of these stories enjoyed the widespread popularity of the tale of Dong Yong,
which combined its moralism with magic and romance. As the story was retold
and restaged, the object of Dong Yong's filial piety moved from his father to
his mother, and the emphasis in the description of his helpmate's divine skill
shifted from quantity to quality. And like the woven brocades Dong Yong's
wife weaves to pay off her husband's debt, the story acquired more and more
complexity: the couple acquires a son, and Dong Yong acquires both an upper-
class wife and a career. The tale of Dong Yong retained its popularity well
into the twentieth century. It even enjoyed a spectacular revival in the 1950s,
when the revised version—the Huangmei Opera's *Married to a Heavenly Immortal*
(*Tianxianpei*)—was turned into a blockbuster movie of the same title.

I. Early References to the Filial Piety of Dong Yong

China's philosophers and thinkers of the fifth to third centuries B.C.E.
occasionally mention filial piety, but for the first treatise exclusively devoted
to filial piety we have to wait for the Western Han dynasty (206 B.C.E.–8 C.E.),
when *The Classic of Filial Piety* (*Xiao jing*) started to circulate. This short work, a
dialogue between Confucius and Zeng Cen, a disciple renowned for his filial
piety, not only extols filial piety as the source of all virtues but also argues
that filial sons make the best bureaucratic officials—the selfless respect for and
obedience to authority that had been inculcated at home made these men the

---

[3] The Chinese scholartree, also known as the Japanese pagoda tree, is the *Sophora japonica*. "This
ornamental tree . . . is found all over China. It often attains a great age, and takes the fantastic shapes
so dear to the Chinese taste. It is venerated and preserved, the branches being supported by posts, and
shrines being placed near the trees" (Shaw, 1914, 255).

[4] Xie, 2000, 487. For complete translations of *The Twenty-Four Exemplars of Filial Piety*, see Chen, 1908,
and Koehn, 1943. Jordan, 1986, provides a full translation preceded by an in-depth analysis.

ideal devoted servants of the throne.[5] By the time of the Eastern Han dynasty (25–220 C.E.), candidates for office had to be recommended to the throne by local officials on the basis of their publicly acknowledged filial piety and incorruptibility. Such a policy resulted in conspicuous displays of filial piety through lavish funerals and mourning rituals, and stories of exemplary filial sons soon started to circulate.[6]

It is in the context of this cult of filial piety that we start to encounter the legend of Dong Yong. Our first evidence of the legend is visual and dates from the second part of the second century. Reliefs depicting the legend show a Dong Yong who out of concern for the well-being of his aged father takes him along in a little cart when he leaves for the fields. The emphasis is on Dong Yong's love and care for his father, and there is as yet no sign of a heavenly helpmate.[7] She is first mentioned in the poem *Numinous Mushroom* (*Lingzhi pian*) by the famous poet Cao Zhi (192–232). This poem, written to praise his brother Cao Pi's establishment of the Wei dynasty (221–265), contains short accounts of a number of filial sons. Cao Zhi summarized the tale of Dong Yong in the following eight lines:

> When Dong Yong's family fell on hard times,
> In his father's old age, all money was exhausted.
> He took out a loan in order to provide for him
> And hired himself out so as to buy delicacies.
>   When creditors arrived at his gate in numbers,
> He was at a loss how to send them off, but
> Heaven's God was moved by his utmost virtue,
> And a divine maiden worked the loom for him.[8]

While Cao Zhi states that Dong Yong was so poor that he hired himself out as a laborer, the poet does not state that Dong Yong sold himself into servitude or that he met his heavenly helpmate while on his way to his master. Those elements are provided only in the accounts of the legend from the fourth century and later, such as the following:

---

[5] The most recent translation of *The Classic of Filial Piety* is provided by Rosemont and Ames, 2009, which includes an extensive introduction. For a bibliographic essay on this text, see Boltz, 1993.

[6] Makeham, 1990.

[7] Wu Hung, 1989, 289–91.

[8] Zhao Youwen, 1985, 327.

Dong Yong at an early age lost his mother. He was living with his father. Whenever he was laboring the fields, he took his father along with him in a deer-drawn cart. When his father died, he sold himself to a rich man in order to provide for the funeral. On his way [to his master] he met with a girl, who called out to him and told him: "I want to be your wife." Subsequently they arrived together at the rich man's place. The rich man said: "Who are you?" She replied: "I am Yong's wife, and I wish to help him repay his debt." The man said: "When you weave three hundred pieces, I will let you go." She had finished them within one ten-day week. When they had gone out of the gate, the girl said to Yong: "I am a daughter of Heaven. Heaven ordered me to help you repay your debt." As soon as she had finished speaking, she disappeared.[9]

A very comparable version of the legend is encountered in Gan Bao's *In Search of the Supernatural* (*Soushen ji*), a well-known collection of miracle tales of the second part of the fourth century.[10] This version of the legend might be called its "classic" account. Through the ages, in an abbreviated or slightly longer form, would be included in all kinds of collections of biographies of filial sons.

From an early date, Dong Yong's divine helpmate has been understood to be Weaving Maiden (*zhinü*). Weaving Maiden (Vega in the constellation Lyra) and Buffalo Boy (*niulang* or *qianniu*, also rendered as Cowherd; Altair) are two stars on opposite sides of the Heavenly River (or Silver River; the Milky Way). Both stars are mentioned together in one of the songs in the ancient *Book of Odes*, which points out that Weaving Maiden and Buffalo Boy do not live up to their names: Weaving Maiden, though working the loom all day, never finishes one piece, and Buffalo Boy (and his beast) never transport a single load. From an early date the two stars were believed to be lovers, who, because of their mutual infatuation, had neglected their duties and, therefore, had been given their separate positions as punishment. Legendary travelers on the Heavenly River would observe Weaving Maiden dutifully working at her loom. Later sources allowed the lovers one meeting each year, on the night of the seventh day of the Seventh Month, when, according to later sources, magpies form a bridge across the Heavenly River for the lovers. In more recent folklore, Weaving Maiden is often said to be the youngest of the seven daughters of the Queen Mother of the West, the heavenly ruler of all female immortals. The love of Weaving Maiden and Buffalo Boy has given rise to a great number of folktales all over China. While these folktales were adapted for the stage in some genres

---

[9]   *Fayuan zhulin*, ch. 62, quoted in Xiang, 1989, p. 227, n. 1. The *Fayuan zhulin* claims its account derives from *The Biographies of Filial Sons* (*Xiaozi zhuan*) by Liu Xiang (79–8 B.C.E.), but it is very unlikely that Liu ever compiled such a work.

[10]   For an English translation, see DeWoskin and Crump, 1996, 14.

of traditional regional theater, they were rarely, if at all, developed into long narrative ballads. Novels on the love of Weaving Maiden and Buffalo Boy were written in premodern times but were not very successful.[11]

II. Buddhism and the Popularization of Filial Piety

While the legend of Dong Yong and Weaving Maiden may well have a folkloric origin, it was part of the elite discourse on filial piety during the early centuries of the first millennium. The large aristocratic families that dominated Chinese society in those years cultivated the virtue of filial piety both to strengthen their cohesion across generations and to claim appointments to political office.[12] The popularization of filial piety among broader segments of the people, however, was indebted to Buddhism. Initially the foreign teaching of Buddhism had been strongly criticized by Chinese opponents for its lack of filial piety: by becoming a monk, a son abandoned his parents and discontinued the family line! In reaction to these attacks, Chinese Buddhism developed its own discourse on filial piety, utilizing the intense emotional bond between mother and son in a typical Chinese family.[13]

The Buddhist discourse on filial piety as it developed over the course of the second part of the first millennium stressed the limitless sufferings that parents, especially mothers, endured in raising a child. Tracts and songs spelled out the extreme sufferings of the mother during pregnancy and nursing. These extensive descriptions were intended to impress on their audience the limitless indebtedness of the child toward his parents, especially the mother, and the impossibility ever to repay them in a befitting manner. At the same time, this Buddhist discourse stressed the inherent sinfulness of the female condition: while a father upon his death may expect to be reborn in heaven, a mother will under normal circumstances be condemned to one of the many hells. Traditional ancestral sacrifices, the Buddhist argument went, were of no benefit to deceased parents at all—they actually were harmful because the slaughter of animals created negative karma. The only way a filial son could save his mother from hell, or at least alleviate her sufferings while there, was by making donations to the Buddhist clergy, especially on the occasion of the Ghost Festival on the fifteenth of the Seventh Month. The Ghost Festival had been instituted to commemorate how the monk Mulian with the aid of the Buddha had saved

---

[11] A more detailed account of the myths and fairy tales about Buffalo Boy and Weaving Maiden is provided in the Appendix.

[12] Knapp, 2005.

[13] Cole, 1998.

his mother from the deepest of hells. While Buddhist sermons addressed to lay patrons praised Mulian as a perfect filial son, they also told the legends of native Chinese filial sons. Because the monastic community depended on patrons' donations for its very survival, it was, in contrast to Confucianism, very much a proselytizing religion, trying to reach the largest possible audience.[14]

It should therefore come as no surprise that the earliest preserved narrative ballad devoted to Dong Yong is found among the so-called transformation texts (*bianwen*) from Dunhuang. During its glory days Dunhuang had been a major city on the Silk Road and a flourishing center of Buddhism. From the fourth to the fourteenth centuries hundreds of Buddhist cave temples were carved out in a cliff some miles from the town. A bricked-up, painted-over side chamber filled with tens of thousands of manuscripts was discovered in one of these cave temples in 1900. Later research showed that this side chamber must have been closed off shortly after the year 1000 (for reasons that are still unclear). The transformation texts found among these manuscripts are vernacular narratives that often but not exclusively focus on Buddhist themes and are intended for performance. Most of these texts are written in alternating prose and verse passages, but a small number are written only in verse, from the beginning to the end. The ballad on Dong Yong is an example of the latter category. The text probably dates from the ninth or tenth century.

In the retelling included in this volume the legend has been extended by providing Dong Yong and his divine spouse with a son who expresses a desire to meet with his mother in heaven. With the help of a fortune-teller (here Sun Bin), the son succeeds in his endeavor, but his enraged mother makes sure that the fortune-teller is punished. As a result, the fortune-teller's books are burned, and ever since that time perfect knowledge of heavenly matters has been impossible for humans. In this version Dong Yong's son is identified as Dong Zhong. Early sources reference a certain Dong Zhong who, by his magical skills, could kill ghosts and humans; he could also feign death and return to life even after a few days, when the worms were coming out of his corpse.

The motif of the young boy who learns, through taunting by classmates, that the mother who has raised him is not his real mother and then sets out to find his real mother is encountered in many later legends, but it is encountered for the first time in the version of the Dong Yong legend provided here. In the later stories, the young boy discovers that his mother has been imprisoned under a mountain or pagoda because of her gluttony and/or lust, acquires

---

[14] The government of later Chinese dynasties such as the Ming (1368–1644) and the Qing (1644–1911) took an increasingly active role in popularizing Confucian values. One of the methods during the Qing was regular public lectures on the Sacred Edict, a set of moral maxims. The first of these maxims focused on filial piety. See Baller, 1924.

magical skills through years of study, and finally frees her from the dungeons of the earth, just as Mulian saved his mother. In the version translated here, however, this motif is combined with the motif of the swan maiden.[15] The young boy learns that his mother is a heavenly fairy who will descend with her sisters to the mythical Anavatapta Pond to take a bath and is instructed by a soothsayer to grab her gown so she will have to show herself to him. This motif is encountered in many other stories, including the modern folktales on Weaving Maiden and Buffalo Boy, in which the young man who steals the immortal's gown imposes his will on her and makes her his wife. Not only is the mother compelled by circumstance to appear nude before her son, but she also must fear that she will be raped by him. Although she is very upset, she punishes the soothsayer instead of her own child. The story would appear to recount the loss of innocence, when a young boy discovers that even his own mother is a sexual being. One is tempted to draw a parallel to the story of Adam and Eve, who have to leave paradise once they become aware of each other's nakedness, or even to the story of Oedipus, who gouges out his eyes once he realizes he married his own mother. Later retellings of the legend of Dong Yong's son looking for his mother, reflecting the theatrical adaptations of the tale, often tone down the sexually explicit nature of the meeting of mother and son.

III. Dong Yong and Weaving Maiden on Stage

Little skits and more elaborate plays may well have been performed in China since time immemorial, but for the emergence of a flourishing dramatic literature we have to wait until the middle of the thirteenth century. At that moment there are two major theatrical genres: the northern plays, or *zaju*, and the southern plays, or *xiwen*. *Zaju* flourished in the commercial theaters of the major northern cities and at court between 1250 and 1450, while *xiwen*, which originated in Wenzhou, were a far more popular genre.

Zaju are relatively short plays. In modern editions they usually consist of four acts, each built around a single suite of arias. In this way, each play tends to focus on the major episodes of the adapted story. Only one actor or actress sang in each individual play, singing the four suites of song, whereas the text of the other characters in the play was limited to prose dialogue. In this way, only one party in the dramatic conflict was allowed to give full expression to his or her feelings. No *zaju* on the legend of Dong Yong has been preserved in its entirety, but a sixteenth-century source preserves a suite of songs that would appear to derive from the second act of a *zaju* on Dong Yong and Weaving

---

[15] On the international distribution of the swan maiden motif, see Miller, 1987.

Maiden. It is clear that the songs are intended to be sung by the actor playing the role of Dong Yong, who at the opening of the act has just buried his mother and is on his way to his master to pay off his debt. The very moment he calls out for his mother, Weaving Maiden appears before him and offers to become his wife. The surprised Dong Yong initially refuses her offer for a variety of moral reasons (and perhaps also fearing that she may be a demon because no proper young lady will offer herself for free), but eventually he gives in to her insistent demand and takes her along. One can easily imagine that this confrontation between a bereaved orphan and an eager teenager may have made for a hilarious number onstage. Even without stage directions and the lines of Weaving Maiden, these songs make for entertaining reading.

Xiwen were much longer plays than *zaju*. Often performed at temple festivals or other community celebrations, they might run to between forty and sixty scenes and take up to one or two days to perform. One reason for their length was that in *xiwen* all actors and actresses were expected to sing, and so the number of arias increased exponentially. No *xiwen* from 1250 to 1450 on the legend of Dong Yong has been preserved, but it has been suggested that a vernacular story entitled *How Dong Yong Met the Female Immortal* (*Dong Yong yu xian zhuan*), which is found in the mid-sixteenth-century collection *Sixty Stories* (*Liushijia xiaoshuo*), may well derive from a *xiwen*. The arguments cited in support of this hypothesis are the vernacular story's frequent shifts between scenes, the brevity of most of the scenes, and the nature of some of the scenes, which include much thinking and planning.[16] In the vernacular story, which probably dates from the fifteenth century, Dong Yong obtains an official post after his master has submitted the brocades of Weaving Maiden to the throne, and he also marries his master's daughter Saijin. Saijin takes care of his son, who now is identified with Dong Zhongshu, a philosopher of the second century B.C.E., who in later legend was credited with supernatural knowledge and magical powers. Again the soothsayer (this time Yan Junping) who assists Dong Zhongshu in finding his birth mother is punished (with blindness), but Dong Zhongshu turns out to be unable to make proper use of the magical gifts of his mother, and this has dire consequences.

By the sixteenth century *xiwen* had developed into a literarily and musically more demanding form known as *chuanqi*, which quickly became the most prestigious and widespread dramatic genre until it was supplanted on the popular stage in the late eighteenth century by the many forms of local opera. Anthologies of individual scenes from *chuanqi* plays that were printed in the

---

[16]   Hanan, 1973, 137–38. Hanan, 1973, p. 129, dates the story to his "middle period" for the composition of vernacular stories (1400–1550). Chinese scholarship usually dates this story to the Song dynasty (960–1278) or the Yuan dynasty (1260–1368).

Wanli period (1574–1619) also include scenes from one or more *chuanqi* on the legend of Dong Yong and Weaving Maiden, which are designated by a variety of titles, such as *Weaving Brocade* (*Zhijin ji*), *Weaving Silk* (*Zhijuan ji*), *Selling Oneself* (*Maishen ji*), and *The Heavenly Immortal* (*Tianxian ji*). By far the most popular scene is the one in which, upon leaving the house of their master, Weaving Maiden takes her leave of Dong Yong to return to heaven. She first suggests the inevitability of their impending separation by a variety of puns and images, but as Dong Yong fails to catch her meaning, she eventually blurts out the truth and ascends to heaven—but not before she has disclosed that she is pregnant. This scene as reproduced in the various anthologies shows major textual differences and appears with different titles but still seems in each case to derive from a single source.

No complete text of such a sixteenth-century *chuanqi* on Dong Yong and Weaving Maiden has been preserved, but *The Comprehensive Catalog with Content Summaries of the Ocean of Song* (*Quhai zongmu tiyao*), a modern compilation based on early eighteenth-century sources, provides a detailed summary of *Weaving Brocade* by a certain Gu Jueyu, who is identified as an actor. Because a *chuanqi* play had to provide parts for all the actors in the company, the "martial male" is given the role of a good friend of Dong Yong who has become a highwayman, whereas the clown is given the role of the master's depraved son who tries to seduce Dong Yong's young and comely helpmate. As the young lover onstage is usually given the characteristics of a student, Dong Yong too is depicted as a young scholar. It is obvious that this *chuanqi* version of the legend has exerted an enormous influence not only on the stage adaptations of the legend in the many genres of local opera all over China but also on the many rewritings in the various genres of narrative ballads and folk epics that have been preserved from the Qing dynasty (1644–1911).[17]

IV. Dong Yong and Weaving Maiden at Xiaogan

In the earliest accounts of the legend of Dong Yong and his heavenly helpmate, the story is clearly set in Shandong province. As the story spread over China, more and more localities claimed to be the place where the events had taken place, often bolstering their credentials by laying claim to the grave of Dong Yong. In the fifteenth-century vernacular story discussed earlier the action has been moved to Jiangsu province. One county in Hubei that prided itself on being the setting of the legend of Dong Yong and Weaving Maiden eventually was named after the event when it was given the official designation of Xiaogan

---

[17] For recent studies of filial piety in the vernacular fiction of the sixteenth century and later, see Epstein, 2006; Tina Lu, 2008, 135–74; and, Shang, 2003, 53–83.

(the miracle of filial piety). Therefore, Xiaogan is mentioned as the setting of the legend in the long nineteenth-century ballad from central China that is translated in this volume. This ballad hails from Hunan province and belongs to the local genre of *wange*. *Wange* are literally "pulling songs," that is, songs that are sung by the men who are pulling a cart with a coffin from the home of the deceased to his grave. In the Hubei-Hunan area *wange* became one of the many designations for the long narrative ballads that were performed at night at the home of the deceased as part of the ceremonies preceding the funeral. In this genre the text consists of stanzas made up of two rhyming seven-syllable lines each. The modern edition of this text on which this translation is based was prepared using two editions from the final years of the Qing dynasty (1644–1911).

Since 1978 the local government of Xiaogan has once again gone to great lengths, by erecting local monuments and publishing popular and scholarly materials, to stress its link to Dong Yong and Weaving Maiden. The popularity of Dong Yong was not limited to Chinese-language areas. He also became a cultural hero among some of the non-Chinese ethnic groups in southern China.[18]

V. The Modern Transformation of Dong Yong and Weaving Maiden

If filial piety was the foundational virtue of imperial China, romantic love became the foundational virtue of modern China in the twentieth century. The modern reformist and revolutionary intellectuals associated with the May Fourth Movement fiercely attacked filial piety, which was condemned as the root of China's backwardness.[19] The modern intellectuals especially criticized the traditional family system, in which, according to them, children were held to absolute obedience to their parents and in which the parents selected the marriage partners of their children, disregarding the wishes of their sons and daughters—often with dire results.[20] Modern intellectuals, including the communists, demanded that young men and women should be free, without any interference from their parents, to marry their one and only true love.[21]

---

[18]   Holm, 2004; Lévi, 1984.

[19]   Chow, 1960. On a more popular level, filial piety continued to be an important value in modern Chinese society. See Ikels, 2004.

[20]   The typical novel on the ills of the traditional family system is Ba Jin's *Family (Jia)* of 1930. For translations, see Pa Chin, 1958, and Pa Chin, 1972.

[21]   Lee, 2007.

Multiple revisions of the marriage law, before and after 1949, were all intended to make "free love" a reality. Whereas some other traditional legends such as the legend of the White Snake and the romance of Liang Shanbo and Zhu Yingtai could easily be reinterpreted to fit this modern ideology, the legend of Dong Yong and Weaving Maiden initially resisted such an easy adaptation into the modernization project. In the early years of the People's Republic of China, however, a drastically rewritten version of the legend enjoyed spectacular popularity.

In his famous "Talks at the Yan'an Conference on Literature and Art" of 1942, Mao Zedong urged writers to make use of traditional forms and genres to spread the revolutionary message among the broad masses of the Chinese population.[22] After the establishment of the People's Republic of China in 1949, this was followed in 1951 with more concrete directives for the revision of traditional plays. On the basis of these directives local cultural cadres set about rewriting *Heavenly Match*, a version of the Dong Yong legend in the repertoire of the Huangmei Opera of Anhui province. They turned Dong Yong from an impoverished scholar into an idealized representative of the exploited peasant class whose filial piety is mentioned only in passing. Rather than starting their play with scenes of Dong Yong caring for his parents or selling himself into servitude, the play now starts with Weaving Maiden and her heavenly sisters utilizing a rare moment of relaxation of the tight control to which they are subjected to observe the hustle and bustle of life on earth. As soon as Weaving Maiden observes the handsome and honest Dong Yong, she decides to descend to earth to assist him in his labors despite his destitution.[23] As she departs, her

---

[22] McDougall, 1980.

[23] In some earlier versions the initiative to descend to the world below would also seem to rest with Weaving Maiden and not with the Jade Emperor, but in such cases she is still moved to do so by Dong Yong's filial piety. See, for instance, the following song to the tune of *Pipoyu* and preserved in a Ming-dynasty anthology:

> Student Dong's filial piety was unequalled:
> He sold his body, buried his mother, and so moved the celestial princess,
>   She wanted with all her heart to be united in wedlock with him.
> By weaving silk she repaid the labor he owed,
> But their affection lasted only a hundred days.
> They met in the shade of the old scholartree,
>   They met in the shade of the old scholartree—
> Oh Heaven,
> And now they part in the shade of the same old tree,
> And now they part in the shade of the same old tree!

> (Du, 1957, 24)

sisters present her with "disaster incense"—if she runs into problems, she will only have to burn this incense and her sisters will come to her aid.

Dong Yong's master and the master's sons are now characterized as typical representatives of the evil landlord class who try to profit maximally from their serfs, but with the help of her sisters Weaving Maiden succeeds within in a single night to complete the impossible assignment imposed on her. By her wit and determination she frees Dong Yong and herself from the clutches of the landlord and his son, but by the time she and Dong Yong are on their way home, her father in heaven has noticed her absence and dispatches a fearsome warrior to the world below to order her to return immediately—if she will not obey, Dong Yong will be smashed to pieces! Seeing no way out, Weaving Maiden thereupon takes her leave of Dong Yong and returns to the palaces of heaven, which to her are like a prison! Set in a generic traditional China, the play, in line with the Marxist ideology of the 1950s, stresses the exploitation of the peasant class by the landlords and the yearning for free love by young men and women—and the impossibility of realizing that yearning in prerevolutionary times.[24] This rewritten version of *Heavenly Match* enjoyed great success onstage. When the play was turned into a movie of the same title in 1955, starring the famous Huangmei Opera diva Yan Fengying (1930–1968), that movie became a true blockbuster and was shown all over China. This success was replicated outside the People's Republic of China by Hong Kong's Shaw Brothers in a 1963 movie entitled *Seventh Heavenly Sister* (*Qixiannü*; English title: *A Maid from Heaven*).

In a comparable way the continuing popularity of the tale of Weaving Maiden and Buffalo Boy was ensured in the second half of the twentieth century by interpreting the tale as a story of true love thwarted by parental authority and class concerns. The tale has repeatedly been adapted for the stage and the screen. In recent years, the annual meeting of the love-struck stars on the night of the seventh of the Seventh Month has been propagated as the Chinese equivalent of Valentine's Day, and the festival is now celebrated in some places with kissing matches.

---

[24]   For an edition of the Chinese text of this play, see Li, 2003, 573–96.

DONG YONG AT DUNHUANG

The following anonymous ballad was found among the roughly fifty thousand manuscripts hidden in the side chamber of a cave temple by monks in Dunhuang (in westernmost Gansu) shortly after the year 1000 and rediscovered in 1900. Among these manuscripts were found numerous examples of narrative texts in the vernacular of the ninth and tenth centuries that are now collectively designated as "transformation texts." Some of the texts are written primarily in prose, many are written in alternating prose and verse (like a chantefable), and a small number are long ballads in seven-syllable rhyming verse. The anonymous ballad about Dong Yong, which has been dubbed The Transformation Text on Dong Yong *by modern Chinese scholars, belongs to this last category. Some scholars, noticing that some of the transitions in the story are rather abrupt, especially in the latter part, have suggested that the text might originally have been composed as a prosimetric text but that, for some reason or other, the prose sections were left out of the copy we have. But as ballads from all over the world can be rather abrupt in their transitions, it does not seem necessary to adopt that hypothesis.*[1]

---

[1]   The translation is based on the edition of the text in Xiang, 1989, pp. 227–37. This text was previously translated into English by Arthur Waley as "The Ballad of Tung Yung," in his *Ballads and Stories from Tun-huang* (1960), pp. 155–62. Waley appends a short discussion on slavery in Dunhuang, illustrated with a translation of a slave contract, very much like the one Dong Yong might have been expected to have signed. Waley and others have noted the similarity between the tale of Dong Yong and his mother and the swan maiden stories in the Western tradition.

I

ANONYMOUS

Human life in this world, if you think of it carefully,
Is just a short moment of noise—what does it matter?
My congregation, be pious of heart and listen intently:
Most important of all it is to be filial to your parents.
  Your good and evil deeds are written down and recorded,
Written down and recorded by the lads of good and evil.[2]
  As for the saints of filial piety, let's talk of Dong Yong:
When he turned fifteen, he had lost both his parents.
  He lamented his poor fate in not having any brothers,
And the tears coursed down from his eyes without end.
Because in all his many lives he had been without sisters,
He had no acquaintances and no relatives by marriage.
  As the family was so destitute, he was without money:
"So I will sell my body in bondage to bury my parents."
Then there soon was a broker who took him along,
And he discussed with him the pious vow he had made.
  A noble man was willing to pay him eighty strings,[3]
While Dong Yong instead wanted a hundred or more.
Having received the money, he took it home with him
And chose and selected a good day for his parents' burial.
  His parents' physical remains were placed in the hall,
And at the head of the coffin pullers he left the house.
At the sight of his parents' corpses, his voice was choked;
He wailed and hollered, weeping loudly, as is the custom.
  The six relatives on this day all gathered to see them off
And followed behind the hearse up to the side of the grave.
When both had been covered and buried and all was done,
Dong Yong wept and cried for both his father and mother.
  And when on the third day the tomb had been raised,
He took leave of his father and mother to pay off his debt.

---

[2] The lads of good and evil are minor divinities who keep a record of the good and bad deeds of every individual. This meticulous account serves as the basis for the rewards and punishments one receives upon one's death, when one is judged by the judges of the underworld.

[3] Traditional Chinese copper coins were round with a square hole in the middle, which allowed them to be strung together. A string of cash counted nominally as a thousand coins, but the actual number was often lower.

When his father and mother saw their son take his leave,
They wished their son good health and a speedy return.
   He took his leave of the neighbors to the east and west
And then set out on his trip of a few miles or more.
On the road he met with a girl who asked him as follows:
"Now you, my young man, from where do you hail?
What is your surname and name? Tell me the truth;
Give me a full and detailed account from the very beginning."
"Young lady, as you ask me this question time and again,
I will give you a detailed account, without any divergence.
   My family originally lived at the foot of Mt. Lang;
There I am known by surname and name as Dong Yong.
All of a sudden my loving mother contracted an illness,
And within a number of days she had lost her life.
   My loving father had died of an illness earlier,
And later it happened that my mother passed on.
On the day of the burial I had no money at all,
So I sold my body in bondage to bury my parents."
   "Why did you not sell the inherited estate and fields?
Why did you insert yourself into the ranks of the lowly?
You did not sell the estate and fields in your possession,
But you left them behind today to serve your master?"
   "It is very kind of you, young lady, to ask about the price,
But I, Dong Yong, do this to repay my parents' kindness."
"Young man, you today practice this filial piety,
And the sight of your filiality has moved Heaven!
'One of your number will go down to the world below,
Will go for a while to that evil realm, that other land!'
This was Indra's[4] personal order to us in his palace:
'I will dispatch you all to help him repay his debt!'
   If you don't reject me as worthless, I'll be yours forever,
And I will come along with you to serve your master."
Dong Yong stepped forward and then knelt down:
"At an early age I lost my parents to my vexation!"
   "What you sold was a single person, that was the deal,
So who is that woman who is standing by the gate?"[5]

---

4   Indra (Tiandi), originally an Indian god, was revered in Chinese Buddhism as the highest god of heaven and a protector of Buddhism.

5   These two lines are spoken by the lender, who does not look forward to having to feed an idle mouth.

Dong Yong answered him by telling him the truth:
"This woman hails from Shades Mountain Township."
   "And what are the skills this woman may possess?"
"She knows the loom and is an expert in pattern weaves."
So the master entrusted her with silk thread;
Altogether she only wanted two roomfuls.
   The master measured out the total amount;
He figured out the value was over a thousand pieces.
The silk thread was all entrusted to her, because she
Knew the loom, was an expert in pattern weaves.
   To begin, she started out by weaving a roll of brocade.
The shuttle's sound shook the earth: blossoms so fragrant!
During the daytime each day she did not do any weaving at all,
But each night she worked the loom—she said it was lucky.
   On the brocade the golden pairs occurred in couples:
Mandarin ducks in pairs matched phoenix couples.[6]
As soon she had woven her brocade, she cut it from the loom;
She folded it neatly and packed it into a chest.
   When the master saw what was stored in the chest,
He considered how this girl could weave patterns.
"This girl certainly is not of this mortal world;
Most likely she was born and raised in heaven!"
   When she had met the number in weaving silks and gauzes,
He set the two of them free to return to their own village.
"Once the two of you have left, have a good journey,
And carry no grudge toward your former master!"
   When the two of them had left, they went on their way.
After yet another ten miles, they would arrive at his estate!
But when they arrived at the place where they had met,
[She said:] "I take my leave to return to heaven's palace!"
   The young woman immediately left on a cloud,
And as she left, she entrusted to him a little baby boy.
All she said was "Take good care of our little baby!"
Dong Yong at this parting was overcome by tears!
   When Dong Zhong had grown up to the age of seven,
He'd play outside on the street, by the side of the road.

---

6   Mandarin ducks are a conventional image for conjugal happiness and loyalty. The Chinese phoenix
is not a solitary, self-regenerating bird. The couple of male and female phoenixes is a common symbol
of lasting love.

The little boy would time and again be cursed and reviled,
As everyone was saying that Dong Zhong had no mother.
  So he ran back home and told his father:
"How come you people have no mother?"
"When I had sold my body in bondage to bury my parents,
I moved a heavenly maiden to help me repay my debt."
  That very moment he was filled with longing for his mother,
And tears flowed down from his eyes without end.
So Dong Yong allowed his son to go search for his mother,
And his son went straightway to master Sun Bin.[7]
  The master consulted the milfoil[8] for his identity:
"This person has come here to search for his mother!
When she comes and takes a bath in the Anavatapta Pond,[9]
You should already have hidden yourself there behind a tree.
  Three women will come, keeping each other company,
And they will rush straightway to the side of the water.
They will take off their heavenly gowns and dive in—
That's when you grasp the purple gown in the middle!"
  This woman turned out to be Dong Zhong's mother,
Who at this time showed herself, ashamed to see her son:
"You, my son, are still too young—how could you know?
It must be because of the divinational skills of Sun Bin!
  Your mother would have loved to keep you and raise you,
But this is not a fitting place for you to live, my son!
Now, take this golden bottle back with you to earth,
And place that golden bottle next to Sun Bin!"

---

[7] Sun Bin is said to have lived during the Warring States period (fourth and third centuries B.C.E.).
He was a pupil of the legendary Master of Ghost Valley (Guiguzi). When Sun Bin was hired by the
king of Wei as a military strategist, a jealous fellow student saw to it that his kneecaps were amputated.
Despite this handicap, Sun Bin later led the troops of Qi to many victories. Military strategy and
prognostication are considered to be closely related skills, and in later centuries Sun Bin acquired a
great reputation as a soothsayer.

[8] Milfoil branches were used in consulting the *Book of Changes*. The number of milfoil branches
obtained by the diviner following a certain procedure would determine whether each of the six lines
of a hexagram would be yin or yang. Once the diviner had in this way identified which of the sixty-
four hexagrams in the *Book of Changes* fitted the situation at hand, he would proceed to explain the
implications of the hexagram.

[9] The Anavatapta Pond is a mythical pond that in Buddhist texts is said to be located to the north
of the Himalayas. Large and surrounded by gold, silver, and precious stones, it was believed to be the
source of the major rivers of this world, such as the Indus and the Ganges.

A sudden explosion appeared before his eyes;
The master lost [his books] as he ran for his life!
He believed that then all of them had been burned,
But when he searched, he still found sixty sheets!
For this reason we don't know the affairs of heaven anymore—
It is all because Dong Zhong had to look for his mother!

A FRAGMENT OF AN EARLY PLAY

Zaju *was the most popular form of drama in northern China from 1250 to 1450 and continued to be performed at court for another century after that, although it was increasingly replaced by so-called southern drama (*xiwen *and* chuanqi*), which had originated south of the Yangzi. In zaju all songs are sung by the leading male or the leading female, who sings four sets of songs, each to a different musical mode. On the basis of these sets, later editors divided zaju into four acts. Each of these acts tends to focus on a single major scene. While some plays have very complicated stage actions, many plays contain acts in which the role of the antagonist is limited to leading questions, which provide the principal male or female with an opportunity to sing his or her arias, expressing emotion in great detail. Such sets of songs also circulated outside the context of the original play.*

The following set of songs in the Shangdiao *mode is contained in the* Yongxi yuefu, *a large compendium of northern arias from the mid-sixteenth century. This set would appear to derive from the second act of an otherwise unrecorded* zaju *adaptation of the legend of Dong Yong and Weaving Maiden, in which the songs were all sung by the leading male. The scene is Dong Yong's sudden meeting with the immortal maiden as he is on his way to his master to start his three years of servitude. In this play the parent he has just buried is his mother, and the very moment he expresses his desire to be able to see her again, the immortal maiden pops up before his eyes, in the middle of the aria to the tune of* Xiaoyaole.[1]

In shifting the focus of Dong Yong's filial piety from his father to his parents, and from there to his mother, the evolution of the legend of Dong Yong reflects a more general development in Chinese filial piety from a strict obedience to the father to an emotional attachment to the mother. In his repeated refusals to accept the immortal maiden as his wife, Dong Yong displays his superior virtue. As many other stories make clear, a man who eagerly accepts the sexual advances of a woman who is not his wife often ends up as the victim of a vicious predator and may well lose his life, so Dong Yong's caution is very prudent. The only proper way for a man and a woman to become husband and wife would be through a marriage that is arranged by a matchmaker. In many later versions the scholartree will speak and serve as the matchmaker for the couple.[2]

---

[1]   Each aria is preceded by the name of the melody to which it is to be sung; the name of the first melody is preceded by the mode to which all the melodies in this suite belong. The melody names are only conventional indications of the tune and have lost all concrete meaning, so I have not translated them and not included the characters in the glossary.

[2]   The following translation is based on Guo Xun, 1981, pp. 2377–80. For a typeset edition, see Li and Dong, 2003, 529–30. Also see Zhao, 1959, 64–5.

ANONYMOUS

[Shangdiao: Jixianbin]

When I think of my parents, bloody tears drip from my eyes:
They've abandoned this lonely child to suffer an orphan's misery.
I don't have any relatives who are like intertwined branches;
Neither do I have good friends who share a single ambition.
When you come, you come bringing sorrow with you;
When you return, you return bringing sorrow along.[3]
I have become a ghost with no refuge and without a grave:
When will there be an end or conclusion to this sad pain?
It moves even the passersby to weep piteously
And also all travelers to be wounded by grief.

[Xiaoyaole]

My dear mother,
You have left me behind without any help or assistance.
As I will work for others as a serf and a slave,
How can I have the Sevens celebrated for you?[4]
I, on my part, seem to be drunk or confused,
And the tears on my cheeks seem to be raked and pushed.[5]
My dear mother,
When will this naughty child be able to see you again?
Who like me knows her—who are you?[6]
You walk up to me and address me by name;
Out of the blue you say we are husband and wife!
If someone here on the road would find out about it—
At present I am wearing mourning—
How could I handle such an accusation!

---

[3] In these two lines Dong Yong is perhaps addressing his shadow, his only companion at this stage.

[4] The Sevens are the Buddhist services for the benefit of the soul of the deceased on the seventh, fourteenth, twenty-first, twenty-eighth, thirty-fifth, forty-second, and forty-ninth days following the person's death.

[5] I do not understand the meaning of "seem to be raked and pushed." Does the author want to say they come in great quantities like leaves that are raked and piled up?

[6] While Dong Yong is mourning his mother, Weaving Maiden suddenly appears in front of him, and the "you" in this line refers to the young girl, not to the mother.

[Cuohulu]

At present I don't have my own farm,
And I lack food and drink.
Because I didn't have the money to bury my mother, I sold my body.
If you would come with me, I'm afraid you would suffer with me,
Because I work for others as a serf or a slave.
To you would apply: "Meeting a chance turned into missing
  a chance!"

[Wuye'er]

You should immediately go back home,
And I will regularly ask for your information.
When my mourning is over, we'll get a matchmaker,
And at that time we will be united in wedlock—
How could such a procedure be deemed too late?
All you talk about is your desire to come with me.
When raising a daughter she should be proper—
Who can believe that you are modest and virtuous?

[Houtinghua]

I here want to rebuff her but without any result;
She makes it even more difficult to let her go.
She there—each and every word is well argued;
Each and every argument is factual.
It really has me filled with grief—
She has no concern for riches and glory!
She is not pressured by some official;
She is not urged on by her parents.
She doesn't scheme for food and drink;
She doesn't hope for riches and glory!

[Shuangyan'er]

How can she want to share my adversities out of the blue?
This makes me even more doubtful.
She must have some connection with my family.
She must owe me a debt from some former life,
And in this life we are reunited once again.

[Cuohulu]

When she hears how I will plow and hoe, she is filled with sorrow;
When I tell her to weave silk and brocade, she is filled with joy.
I see that she is retiring and yielding without second thoughts.
When your three hundred bolts of silk and brocade are done,
He will say that it really was not an easy task,
That this arduous suffering was no light matter.

[Langlilai sha]

You say you are willing to be a slave and work as a laborer;
You say you want to set me free and buy out my contract.
That Zhuo Wenjun long ago was not an exceptional person—
Which woman in past or present resembles you?[7]
If one day by any chance I will enjoy riches and glory,
I'll make sure to make it up to you, my darling wife!

---

[7]   Zhuo Wenjun was a rich young widow when she eloped with the destitute poet Sima Xiangru.

DONG YONG &
DONG ZHONGSHU

Well-developed vernacular stories (huaben) *written in prose interspersed with poems, lyrics, and couplets have already been found among the manuscripts from Dunhuang. The genre continued to be practiced in later centuries, but texts from the Song dynasty rarely survived. Most of the earliest stories that have come down to us date only from the centuries following the Song, and the earliest known (partially preserved) printed collection of vernacular stories dates only from the mid-sixteenth century, when Hong Bian compiled and published the* Stories from the Pure Level Mountain Hall (Qingping shantang huaben), *also known as* Sixty Stories (Liushijia xiaoshuo). How Dong Yong Met the Immortal, *which is contained in that collection, probably dates from 1400 to 1550.*

One of the reasons to attribute the story to such a late date is that some of its characteristics—such as the frequent shifts between scenes, the brevity of most of the scenes, and the nature of some of the scenes (including much thinking and planning)—strongly suggest that this version of the legend was based on an earlier adaptation as a xiwen, *a type of musical play that originated in the thirteenth century in Wenzhou and from there became popular throughout the eastern part of the Yangzi Valley.*[1]

---

[1]   The following translation is based on the edition of the text in Hong Bian, 1957, 235–44. A French translation may be found in Dars, 1987, 66–82.

ANONYMOUS

How Dong Yong Met the Immortal

Introduction to the Story

He mortgaged his body to bury his father
And was not ashamed to work the land as a laborer.
His filial piety moved a divine immortal to descend—
Broad and expansive, the blessings were grand.

Our story goes that during the Zhonghe reign period of the Eastern Han dynasty,[2] in Dong's Scholartree Village of Danyang County of Runzhou Prefecture in Huai'an, there lived a man called Dong Yong, with the style Yanping, of twenty-five years of age. In his youth he had studied the Odes and Documents,[3] but at a very early age he had lost his mother. Only his father was left, and he was over sixty. The family was poor, so he devoted himself to farming. He was wont to bring his father in a little cart and leave him by the side of the field in the shade of a tree, and he would feed his father from the proceeds of his labor. This was how greatly filial he was.

It happened that the area was struck by a devastating drought: smoke rose up from the wells, treetops burst into fire, and grain became so exceedingly expensive that you couldn't buy it anywhere even if you had the money! Dong Yong thought to himself: "[A few] miles from here lives a certain Gentleman Fu whose only aim is to assist the poor and save them from suffering. I'll have to go to him to ask for help." So he said to his father: "Because of this famine, there's no food to be found, and also the weather is freezing cold, so I want to go to Gentleman Fu's place to borrow some rice and money in order to survive." His father said: "Please go, but come back immediately, whether you can borrow something or not, so I don't have to worry."

When Dong Yong had taken leave of his father, he left, turning every three steps into two. At that time it was the middle of the Twelfth Month: the ground

---

[2] There is no Zhonghe reign period in the Eastern Han. We later learn that the capital is at Chang'an, so the author may have intended the Zhongyuan reign period (156–150 B.C.E.) or the Zhenghe reign period (96–93 B.C.E.) of the Eastern Han.

[3] The "Odes" refers to the *Book of Odes*, the "Documents" to the *Book of Documents*. These are two of the Five Classics. Here they refer more generally to the classical texts studied in school in preparation for an official career.

was frozen, the air was freezing, and a fierce northwestern wind was blowing. While his stomach was rumbling and his body was shivering, he walked on despite the hunger and cold, and against his expectations a heavy snow started to fall, whirling and swirling, fluttering and flying.

> They call it all a sign of a good harvest,
> But what about such signs of a good harvest?
> Here in the capital the poor are many:
> To them, the sign is best if not too heavy.

Now our story takes another direction: it tells that Gentleman Fu, at that very moment at home with his wife, was enjoying the snow. When this gentleman saw how heavily the snow was coming down, he ordered his servant Wang Tong to get a thousand strings of cash from the strong room and to fetch ten *dan* of grain[4] from the storeroom to distribute in front of the gate—whether man or woman, everyone was to get relief. At that time Dong Yong also arrived at the gate and saw the distribution of money and rice. He thereupon received ten strings of cash and one *dan* of rice, and after he had thanked the gentleman, he returned as fast as fire. Here applied:

> If you request help, request it from a true philanthropist;
> If you assist others, assist the have-nots in time of need.

Battling the snowstorm Dong Yong went back home with the money and rice, and when the father saw his son return, he was overcome with joy. With the money Dong Yong bought some firewood and rice and started up a fire for his father. When they had cooked the rice and eaten it, they saw that the snow was falling even heavier as the evening arrived. Here applied:

> Flakes as big as a fist were dancing through the sky:
> Travelers on the road could only bitterly complain.

When father and son had managed to get through another half month or so, the father fell ill because of the sufferings of hunger and cold, and once he had taken to bed, he would not rise. Dong Yong was greatly suffering in his heart and wanted to invite a physician to cure him, but he didn't have any money anymore. He hoped his father would scrape through and recover, but unexpectedly his father passed away after having been ill for five or six days. Dong Yong wept piteously without end and repeatedly fainted. Truly,

---

[4]   A *dan* is a weight measure of over a hundred pounds.

Your roof is leaking, and right then it rains night after night;
You are traveling by boat and then run into a stiff headwind.

When his father had died, Dong Yong was completely bereft of means, so he thought: "I only have my uncle on my mother's side who is living in the eastern village, so I can only go to him for help and borrow some money to buy a coffin." Immediately he went to the house of his uncle and told him that he had lost his father and lacked money. When his uncle heard this, he also had no ready cash, so he let Dong Yong have two bolts of linen and one bolt of silk as a loan. Dong Yong exchanged those for a coffin and, upon his return, put it on display at home. From early till late he wept and cried, and during the daytime he plowed and sowed for others in order to survive. He wanted to give his father a proper burial, but again he lacked the money needed for that purpose.

Light and shadow quickly passed by, and suddenly already more than a year had passed. As he did not have the money for a burial, he came up with a plan: "I will have to sell my body to others and work for them as a bonded laborer, and once I have that money, I will make the announcement." That very day he left his house and went straightway to the house of Gentleman Fu, and when he had greeted the servant, he asked him to tell his master that he wanted to sell himself. Gentleman Fu emerged from the hall and called Dong Yong inside to question him in detail. Dong Yong said: "My name is Dong Yong, and I hail from Dong's Scholartree Village in Danyang County. At an early age I lost my mother. This year I also lost my father. The coffin is stored at home, and I have no money for a proper funeral. Today I have come here on purpose to pray for your help. I am freely willing to sell myself to you. I want a thousand strings of cash to go back home to bury my father, and then I will promptly come back to your house to work as a bonded laborer for three years. I hope and pray that you in your compassion will come to my aid!" When the gentleman heard this, he said: "You are an extremely filial person!" He told his servant to get a thousand strings of cash and hand them to Dong Yong, and the latter thanked the gentleman with a bow and went out through the gate. Here applied:

From the clouds he stretched out his cloud-grabbing hand
To raise up the man who was snared in the web of heaven.

When Dong Yong had come home with the money, he hired some fellow-villagers the next day to carry the coffin to the ancestral grave plot in the southern hills. When the burial was completed, he spent a night there, and the next day packed all the luggage he could carry. After he had locked the main gate, he set out on his trip, walking along. When he arrived at the foot of a large tree, he rested there for a while, and before he had noticed, he had fallen asleep under that tree.

But our story goes that Dong Yong's filial piety had even moved the court of heaven. The Jade Emperor[5] noticed him from afar and thereupon ordered the heavenly immortal Weaving Maiden to descend to the mortal world, become Dong Yong's wife, and help him pay back his debt by weaving silk—when her work was done after a hundred days, she was to ascend to heaven as before. Immediately when Weaving Maiden had received this order, she descended at the foot of that scholartree.[6]

When Dong Yong woke up and raised his head, he saw a girl with the following features:

> The goddess of the moon, Chang'e, could not compare;
> A beauty born in highest heaven, hard to paint:
> Her jade white face was prettier than Precious Consort Yang;[7]
> Her myriad charms worked wonders without end.
>
> When she would walk, her willow waist moved graciously;
> Her autumn waves were just like rivers, far and distant.[8]
> Her golden lilies, tender sprouts, measured three inches only,[9]
> A purity that shamed the flowers, hid the moon!

When that girl opened her one dot of red lips, she displayed two rows of fragments of jade as she stepped forward and greeted him, asking him: "Young man, what brings you here?" Dong Yong greeted her in turn and said: "My name is Dong Yong, and I hail from Dong's Scholartree Village. In my early youth I lost my mother, and last year I lost my father. Because the coffin was still stored at home and I was incapable of providing him with a proper funeral, I sold myself. Now that I have buried my father, I am on my way to Gentleman Fu to repay my debt. Tired from walking, I rested here for a while. Because you so kindly asked me, I've told you all the facts." When he was finished speaking, tears coursed down his cheeks. The immortal maiden said: "So you are such a filial person! Now please listen to what I have to say. I hail from Gourong

---

5   From the Song dynasty (960–1278) on, the Jade Emperor (Yudi) was widely venerated as the head of the bureaucratically organized pantheon of Chinese popular religion.

6   For a definition of the Chinese Scholartree, see p.xiv, note 3.

7   Precious Consort Yang is Yang Guifei, the favorite concubine of Emperor Xuanzong (reg. 712–756).

8   "Autumn waves" are a conventional image for the eyes.

9   The Chinese text translates literally as "generating ten toes," which does not seem to make sense. I have replaced that phrase with "measured three inches only," the standard praise of bound feet.

County, and my parents and parents-in-law have all died. To my misfortune, my late husband has also passed away and I find it hard to make a living, so I am looking for a good-hearted man to marry and serve happily." Dong Yong said: "Young lady, take your ease, but I have to leave." The immortal maiden said: "Now I see that you are such a filial person, I truly want to marry you as your wife and accompany you to the Fu family to repay your debt. How do you feel about that?" Dong Yong replied: "Young lady, that's very kind of you. But as there is no matchmaker, it can't be done." The immortal maiden said: "Why don't we ask this scholartree to act as matchmaker if we do not have a matchmaker?"

Dong Yong rebuffed her time and again till the immortal maiden became angry and said: "I am not some slut! The reason I want to marry you is because I see that you are such a filial person! But you are opposed and rebuff me! You must have heard this saying of the ancients: when there exists an affinity, couples can meet despite a distance of a thousand miles; without such an affinity, couples will not see each other even when face-to-face. This is also such a case of karmic affinity, so why do you have these misgivings?"

Dong Yong saw no other solution but to marry her as his wife, and holding hands, they walked on. He then said: "Some days ago I told Gentleman Fu only that I would work three years as a laborer to pay off the debt. When he now sees the two of us enter his gate, I'm afraid he'll be annoyed." But the immortal maiden said: "Don't worry. From my earliest youth I've learned to weave all kinds of silk and cotton, so he will be very pleased."

When they eventually arrived at the gentleman's place, the two of them greeted him with a bow, and Dong Yong informed him he had come with his wife who could weave. The gentleman was greatly pleased and promptly asked: "How much thread do you want?" The immortal maiden said: "To begin with, I want ten pounds, and in a single day, I will weave ten bolts." When he heard this, the gentleman said: "I don't believe that! You are not going to tell me you have a hundred hands? But if this is the way you want it, I will have you weave three hundred bolts of satin, and then I will let you go back." He immediately gave her ten pounds of thread and told Dong Yong and his wife to go and weave. In one day and one night they indeed completed the weaving of ten bolts of satin and presented these to the gentleman. The gentleman and his whole family, young and old, were surprised: "We have never seen anyone who worked so fast!" Actually, at night the immortal maiden had the other immortal maidens come down and help her with her weaving, and that is why she could weave so quickly.

Light and shadow are like snapping your fingers: within one month she had woven over three hundred bolts of satin, which they presented to the gentleman. The latter was greatly pleased and praised her, saying: "Such a woman is rarely found in this world!" He then asked Dong Yong: "Your wife cannot be a mortal being, because if she were a mortal being, how would she be able to weave three hundred bolts of satin in a single month?" Dong Yong answered him: "I will be honest with you. I ran into this woman while on the road, and when she heard me tell about my filial piety, she promptly wanted to marry me and help me pay back my debt." The gentleman said: "So that's what happened! You truly brought this miracle about by your filial piety. Initially we said that you would work as a laborer for three years, but now it's all done in three months. I will give you ten ounces of gold to take with you and start some business."

Dong Yong promptly thanked the gentleman with a bow, and with his wife he went away. When they arrived at the foot of the scholartree where they had met in the beginning, they rested there for a while. The immortal maiden said: "At that time you and I became husband and wife at the foot of this scholartree, and now three months have passed!" Suddenly tears coursed down her cheeks. When Dong Yong asked his dear wife why she cried, the immortal maiden said: "Today the karmic affinity between you and me has come to an end, and that's why I am so depressed. I will be honest with you: I am no one else but Weaving Maiden. The Emperor on High pitied you because of your filial piety and dispatched me to go down to earth to become your wife and help you pay back your debt. The hundred days are fulfilled. I am now one month pregnant. If I give birth to a girl, I will keep her with me in the palaces of heaven, but if I give birth to a boy, I will send him down to you. You will later rise to a high position, but you are not allowed to divulge the secrets of heaven." When she was finished speaking, auspicious clouds arose under her feet and slowly she rose upward. Dong Yong wished to keep her with him but didn't know how and loudly wept to heaven: "I had hoped we would live together as husband and wife till our old age—who could have known we would be separated halfway?" When he was done weeping, he straightway went back, and when he arrived in front of [his father's] grave, he wept again and built a hut of straw to guard the grave mound, but we will not talk about that.

Now let us tell that when Gentleman Fu was at home and had nothing else to do, he opened the bolts of satin the immortal maiden had produced, and they all showed dragon and phoenix patterns while their brilliance outshone the sun and moon. The gentleman was greatly surprised and didn't dare keep this a secret, so he reported the affair to the local prefect. When the local prefect learned through questioning about the miracle due to filial piety, he drafted a memorial and sent it up to the court. And when the Son of Heaven of the Han dynasty perused this memorial, his dragon mien showed his great pleasure: "Ever since We have ascended the throne, there have repeatedly been cases of great filiality, but there has never been a man displaying such exceptional filial piety!" Thereupon he ordered his courtiers to compose an edict, summoning Dong Yong to court.

That very day the imperial envoy arrived in Runzhou, and the prefect ordered his staff to invite Dong Yong. When the latter arrived at the prefecture, he received him most courteously, to the great surprise of Dong Yong, who bowed down and said: "I am only an insignificant nobody without any special virtue or ability, so how could I dare bother Your Excellency to show me such respect?" The prefect said: "Don't be so modest! Your Honor is a man of exceptional filial piety, and we have here an edict of the Son of Heaven!" The imperial envoy then brought out the edict, which he opened and recited, while Dong Yong and the prefect knelt down and listened. The edict read:

A Summons of the August Emperor
Who Obeys Heaven and Continues the Cycle

To be loyal as a vassal and to be filial as a son constitutes the great norm of the way of humans and constitutes the essential teaching for being a man. Therefore, those who are loyal serve as measure and balance of state and nation, and those who are filial become the precious vessels for ordering the family.

From the report of the prefecture of Runzhou We now have learned of the filial piety of Dong Yong. While he originated from bramble fences, he yet grasped the great meaning of *The Classic of Filial Piety*, and even though he suffered numerous adversities, he yet maintained a mind of joy in servitude. Is this not a sign that Our Dynasty will be restored to greatness? And yet such a filial son originated in the outlying provinces!

On the day of the arrival of this summons order Dong Yong is to proceed immediately to the imperial palace so he may be appointed to office upon an evaluation of his talents. Wouldn't that be a stimulus for future developments?

Respect this order!

When Dong Yong had listened to the end, and after he had expressed his gratitude in the direction of the palace, he asked the imperial envoy to take his rest in the post station. Dong Yong went back home and said good-bye to relatives and neighbors. On the next day, he took his leave of the local prefect, and with the imperial envoy he set out on his journey. Here applies:

Summoned by imperial edict to come to the national capital,
One spurs on one's horse with the whip, not daring to tarry.
The apricot flowers display the same red for over ten miles;
Satisfied in the spring breeze—one's horse running lightly!

After a number of days, when Dong Yong and the imperial envoy had arrived at the capital, the courtiers presented him to the Son of Heaven of the Han. The Son of Heaven was greatly pleased and appointed him as president of the ministry of war, whereupon he took on his office, but no more about that.

Let's tell that Gentleman Fu was also appointed by the court to the office of an assistant judge because he had presented such exceptional satin to the throne. The gentleman had a daughter, who was called Saijin. She was very pretty but had not yet been betrothed. That day the gentleman proposed to his wife: "Wouldn't it be a good idea to bring in Dong Yong as Saijin's husband?" Thereupon they asked a matchmaker to propose this to Dong Yong. When Dong Yong heard this, he was extremely pleased, and he said: "I have not yet been able to repay his earlier favors, and if he now makes me his son-in-law, his favors are even more unforgettable." So he told the matchmaker to respectfully report to Gentleman Fu that he was only too happy to accept the proposal. When they had selected a lucky hour, they exchanged betrothal gifts, and the wedding took place. Here applies:

A clear breeze and a bright moon: these go well with each other.
A pretty girl and a smart boy are the finest match in this world:
"In the sky we want to be birds that soar up on shared wings;
In the grave we want to grow into trees with linked branches."

But let's not talk about the harmonious marriage of President Dong and his wife. Let's tell how in the heavenly palace after her separation from Dong Yong, when the nine months had quickly passed, Weaving Maiden gave birth to a boy. When he had lived to one month, she chose a name and called him Dong Zhongshu. Thereupon she took him to the world below so Dong Yong could raise him.

Let's tell that President Dong went to his office and saw a woman standing in the entranceway. President Dong ordered his underlings to scare her away: "Who are you, woman, that you dare to spy on an official of the court?" But the immortal maiden loudly shouted: "Have you forgotten how I helped you by weaving silk that you now try to scare me off?" When Dong Yong heard this and hastily descended from his hall, she turned out to be his former wife. Greatly surprised, he embraced her and wept, and then he asked her: "What is the reason, my dear wife, that you have been so kind as to descend to this world? And who are you carrying in your arms?" The immortal maiden said: "That is your son. I have come today for the very purpose of delivering him to you." Dong Yong expressed his gratitude with a bow and said: "My dear wife, I am deeply grateful for your kindness. Did you already choose a name for him?" The immortal maiden said: "The Jade Emperor has already chosen a name for him, and he is called Zhongshu."

Dong Yong was greatly pleased, and once he had taken the baby in his arms, he said: "More than a year has already gone by since our separation. Now that we meet again today, I should enjoy this glory and splendor with you, staying with you for the rest of our lives." The immortal maiden said with a smile: "My dear husband, you are mistaken. Husband and wife have their heavenly fate, and I am not allowed to stay for long." When she had finished speaking, clouds arose under her feet, and she slowly rose up into the sky. President Dong wept loudly, facing heaven, and when his wife, lady Fu, heard this and came outside to have a look, she promptly asked: "My dear husband, why are you so depressed? And who are you carrying in your arms?" Dong Yong told her everything that had happened. Her Ladyship was very pleased and ordered a wet nurse to take care of the baby.

Light and shadow are just like snapping your fingers. Here applies:

> The crow flies on and on, and the hare never rests;[10]
> Morning comes and evening goes, without any end.
> Nüwa was able to produce stones to mend the sky,[11]
> But she cannot make a glue to fasten sun and moon!

All of a sudden more than twelve years had passed, and Dong Zhongshu had reached the age of twelve. His parents had him go to school to study the books, and he became conversant with the Nine Classics and the books and histories. Suddenly one day, when he was studying his books in the academy, a little kid who was a fellow student cursed Zhongshu by calling him "a motherless child." When Zhongshu was cursed in this way, he didn't dare reply but straightway went home, and when he saw President Dong, he grabbed his gown and started to weep loudly: "Why do all other people curse me by calling me a motherless child? Today I want to get to the bottom of the matter! I insist on seeing the mother who gave birth to me!" President Dong then said: "Your mother is an immortal maiden from the palaces of heaven, so how could you see her?" When Zhongshu heard this, he wept even louder, saying: "If I could only see

---

10   The sun is inhabited by a three-legged crow, while the moon is inhabited by a hare.

11   When the sky collapsed after the demon Gonggong had broken one of the pillars separating heaven and earth, the goddess Nüwa produced the stones that were used to repair the dome of heaven.

my mother, I would be happy even if it would mean my death! If you say I will never be able to see her, I will commit suicide right here and now!" President Dong said: "My child, don't be so upset! On the market of Chang'an here you can find the fortune-teller Yan Junping who can know the past and the future.[12] Go and ask him!"

When Zhongshu heard this, he promptly left with ten copper coins to have his fortune told. Yan Junping asked him: "Young man, on what subject would you like to question the hexagrams?" Zhongshu told him that he wanted to see his mother: "So I hope that you, master, will show me a way." When the master had consulted the hexagrams, he said: "Your mother is a heavenly immortal, Weaving Maiden! How would it be possible to see her?" When Zhongshu heard this, he wept and bowed down on the ground: "Master, if you by any chance will show me a way, I will never forget your favor in life or in death!" The master replied: "Such filial piety is rare indeed, so I will tell you a way. On the seventh day of the Seventh Month, your mother will descend together with the other immortal maidens on Great White Mountain to collect herbs.[13] She is number seven, dressed in yellow." Zhongshu asked: "How far is it from here to Great White Mountain?" The master replied: "About three thousand miles!" Zhongshu also asked: "Will my mother be willing to recognize me as her son when I get there?" The master said: "You grasp the gown of the one dressed in yellow, kneel down, and weep, and she will recognize you. But if she asks you which person told you this, you on no account can tell her it was me!"

Zhongshu left after having paid the master and thanking him with a bow. He straightway returned to the mansion, and when he saw his parents, he told them: "Master Yan told me to go to Great White Mountain to meet my mother, so today I will take my leave and set out." President Dong said: "It's more than three thousand miles from here to Great White Mountain, and there are many tigers and wolves! My child, you are still so young—how could you go there?" But Zhongshu said: "I will have no regret even if I die. I am determined to go."

When President Dong saw that he was dead set on going, he could only tell Old Wang to provide him with travel money and accompany his child. That very day Zhongshu said good-bye and set out on his journey. While on the road, he would eat when hungry and drink when thirsty, stop for the night and set out at dawn. After many days, they arrived at the foot of a mountain,

---

[12] Yan Junping lived in the final decades of the first century B.C.E. in Chengdu, where he established a reputation as a soothsayer. In our story Yan knows what is hidden by consulting the hexagrams in the *Book of Changes*.

[13] The Great White Mountain (Taibaishan) is one of the highest peaks in the Qinling range to the southwest of Xi'an. Here the name does not refer to an actual mountain, however, but to a mythical place far, far away.

and when they asked, it turned out to be Great White Mountain. When they had crossed the first mountain ridge, they saw wild deer carrying flowers and mountain gibbons offering fruits, and when they crossed yet another mountain ridge, they saw fresh flowers and green grasses in wild profusion and a waterfall that came tumbling down.

This just happened to be the seventh day of the Seventh Month, so suddenly Zhongshu saw a group of immortal ladies come down and wash their herb bottles. He promptly told Old Wang to hide himself and hastily rushed forward. He fell on his knees and bowed down in front of the number seven, dressed in yellow, and as he grasped her gown, he cried: "Mother, how could you be so cruel as to abandon me?"

The immortal maiden asked: "Little boy, who are you? And who told you to come here?" Zhongshu answered: "I am your son, Dong Zhongshu, and my father told me to come and pay my respect to you, mother!" The immortal maiden said: "My child, quickly go back. There are many wolves here that devour people, so you can't stay here any longer." Zhongshu said: "I have come here across a thousand mountains and myriad rivers, so how can you just tell me to get lost?" The immortal maiden said: "No matter how hard it may be to deny my motherly feelings, I am still afraid that Heaven may come to know of this, and then my punishment will not be light. You must go back and tell your father to take good care of himself. This must be because that old geezer Yan Junping couldn't keep his mouth shut and told you to come here. Now take this golden bottle and hand it over to Master Yan to thank him for his efficacious hexagrams. I also give you a silver bottle. In this bottle there are a few grains of rice, but when you are back, you can only eat one grain every day—on no account can you eat more!"

When she had finished speaking, clouds arose below her feet, and the immortal maidens all slowly rose into the sky. Zhongshu wanted to keep her down, but she had already gone too far, so he could only weep loudly, facing heaven. When Old Wang heard this, he hastily came over, and after he had comforted him, they shouldered their luggage and returned quickly. When after many days they had arrived in Chang'an, Zhongshu greeted his parents and told them the whole story of his meeting with his mother: "She repeatedly sent her best wishes to you, my father. She gave me this golden bottle for Master Yan. And this silver bottle she gave to me for fun." President Dong was very pleased and said: "As she gave you this golden bottle for Master Yan, you can't disappoint her, so quickly take it to him!"

Zhongshu immediately went with the golden bottle to the house of Master Yan. The master was sitting in front of the gate. After Zhongshu had bowed to the master, he handed him the golden bottle, saying: "My mother sends you her best wishes, master, and as she has nothing else to express her gratitude, she sends you this golden bottle."

When the master had taken it from him and inspected it, its brilliance dazzled even the sun. He did not say a word but thought to himself: "This is the greatest treasure on earth, rarely seen by man, as it is the Golden Tranquility Bottle from the heavenly palace." He looked at it from all sides, but when he took out the stop of the bottle, he was in for quite a surprise. A spark of fire came out through the opening of the bottle and completely burned to ashes all his books about lucky dates and numerology and knowing the past and the future. When the master frantically tried to extinguish the fire, the smoke blew into his face and suddenly caused both his eyes to go blind. This is the beginning of the tradition of blind people memorizing books of numerology.

Zhongshu was dumbstruck with fright and hurried back home. When he poured out the grains of rice of his silver bottle, he found he had about seven cups, so he burst out in laughter: "My mother told me to eat only one grain each day, but how could that fill me up? I'd better cook and eat this rice in one go." Who could have known in the one, two, three days after eating this rice, his body would become long and big, huge and fat! Even though he did not eat anything, he still felt no hunger, and within half a month his body had grown to ten feet and his waist measured ten spans. He was perplexed by this and at night could not sleep, but there was no medicine that could undo the effect.

When his father and mother saw him like this, they were frightened. And who could have expected that his father Dong Yong, because of this fright and because he was old and sickly, would fall ill and die?

When Zhongshu saw that his father had passed away, he was overcome by grief. He dressed him in a shroud and put him in a coffin and then brought the hearse back to his home village. When the funeral was completed, he filially guarded the grave for three years, without any thought of food or drink. Then suddenly one day he told people: "Earlier my mother gave me this rice of the immortals, but in my ignorance I ate it all in one go, so I unexpectedly got this weird body. Now the Jade Emperor has dispatched the Fire Light Generalissimo to summon me to heaven, where I have been appointed to the office of god of the cranes. On the days *renchen* and *guisi* I will ascend to heaven, and from [*ji*]*gai* to [*yi*]*si* I will journey to the west.[14] After I have returned to the northeastern region for forty-four days, I will again ascend to heaven for sixteen days." Right down to today, for a myriad of years, he has been the god of cranes in the retinue of the Great Year.[15]

---

[14]   From *renchen* to *yisi* covers a period of fourteen days. The ten characters that form the Heavenly Stems and the twelve characters that form the Earthly Branches are combined to form a series of sixty bisyllabic terms, which are used to count years, months, days, and hours. Here they are used to count days.

[15]   Great Year is the hypothetical planet Anti-Saturnus, which circles the sun every twelve years. Great Year is one of the most fearsome astral deities.

WEAVING BROCADE

The popularity of Gu Jueyu's Weaving Brocade, or at least of the scene of the parting of Dong Yong and his heavenly helpmate, is attested to by the many drama anthologies of the Wanli period (1573–1619) that contain this scene. The translation of the parting scene presented here is based on the version of the text in the Newly Printed Currently Popular Songs and Arias from North and South: A Comprehensive Selection of a Myriad of Tunes (Xinjuan Nanbei shishang yuefu yadiao Wanqu hexuan).[1]

The full text of Weaving Brocade, however, has not been preserved. The title was listed by Qi Biaojia (1602–1645) in his catalog of chuanqi plays, Classified Plays of the Distant Mountain Hall (Yuanshantang qupin), but his comments are limited to a short summary of the contents, an assertion of the truth of Dong Yong's meeting with Weaving Maiden, and the remark that Dong Zhongshu could not have been Dong Yong's son.[2]

A more detailed entry on Weaving Brocade is found in The Comprehensive Catalog with Content Summaries of the Ocean of Song (Quhai zongmu tiyao).[3] The learned scholars who compiled this work did not hesitate to express their disgust at the way popular tradition had transformed "the facts" of history! Individual entries in The Comprehensive Catalog with Content Summaries of the Ocean of Song focus on a summary of the contents of the play and a discussion of the origin of these materials. Information on authorship and editions may be provided too. Following the translation of the parting scene, this volume presents a full translation of the entry on Weaving Brocade in The Comprehensive Catalog with Content Summaries of the Ocean of Song.[4]

---

[1] A typeset edition of the text is provided in Li and Dong, 2003, 531–9.

[2] Qi, 1955, 145.

[3] This work, first published in 1928, is based on an earlier anonymous work entitled Researches on and Summaries of Plays (Yuefu kaolüe), which was probably completed between 1715 and 1722. It also includes information from a similar work, called Collected Researches on Southern Plays (Chuanqi huikao), of roughly the same period. But the title was borrowed from a huge catalog of plays compiled later in the eighteenth century by Huang Wenchang (b. 1736), entitled Catalog of the Ocean of Song (Quhai mu).

[4] The translation is based on Quhai zongmu tiyao, 1959, 1190–2.

GU JUEYU

The Parting at the Scholartree

(Huaiyin fenbie)

[Langtaosha]

(Dong Yong)
With hurried steps I walk on ahead
To the shade of the lush scholartree:
Verdant and emerald, its green so rich!
Putting down my luggage, I stop here
And wait for my wife,
And wait for my wife.

[To the same tune]

(Weaving Maiden)
As soon as I left the rich man's gate,
I found it hard to walk on my bound feet,
And when I lifted my head, I didn't see my husband.
He for his part went happily on ahead,
Not knowing that we today will be parted again,
Not knowing that we today will be parted again!

(Dong Yong) My wife, there you are!

(Weaving Maiden) How unfaithful you are! You didn't even wait for me!

(Dong Yong) I was waiting for you here. What took you so long?

(Weaving Maiden) When I was saying good-bye to Miss Saijin, I couldn't bear to leave her; that's why it took so long. Where are we here?

(Dong Yong) We are here at the foot of the scholartree, the place where I first met you. Darling, I have no other way to display my gratitude than to express my thanks with a bow.

[To the same tune]

(Dong Yong)
With a deep bow I thank the scholartree:
Dear scholartree, you were our matchmaker.
I thank you for your great benefaction:
The debt of three years today is paid off.
As soon as I raise the subject,
I am filled with happy joy;
As soon as I raise the subject,
I am filled with happy joy!

[To the same tune]

(Weaving Maiden)
He over there is filled with happy joy,
While I over here cry more and more tears:
Husband and wife are so close to each other,
But I have to ascend to the heavenly court!

(Dong Yong) Darling, why are you talking about tears?

(Weaving Maiden)
I'm worried that I cannot walk on bound feet in lotus shoes:
How can I manage the mountain roads and river crossings?
Darling Dong, my feet are hurting from walking;
I cannot go any farther!

(Dong Yong) I get it, you want to sit down for a while, but how could you sit down on the ground? Let me find a rock for you to sit on.

(Weaving Maiden) I will also find one for you so we can sit together for a while—wouldn't that be wonderful?

(Dong Yong) Darling, you have been such a great help to me these last days, and we also have become a married couple for the rest of our lives. I would not be able to pay you back these benefactions even if I could tie straw or bring a bracelet.[5]

(Weaving Maiden) Darling, the young mistress has been so kind as to give me a few feet of shoe covering and ten ounces of silver in two pieces of sterling silver

---

[5] This line refers to two stories: a man was once saved from death when the deceased father of a concubine he had saved from death made his enemy trip with a straw rope; the other story describes the gratitude of a bird to a hunter who releases him.

that seems to come from the same ingot.[6] Please take all of this.

(Dong Yong) Why do you say so? You should keep what the young mistress has given to you. Why should I take it?

(Weaving Maiden) I have no use for any silver.

(Dong Yong) Darling, you are mistaken! How can silver be useless? Tomorrow you should go out and buy stuff.

(Weaving Maiden) Darling, if I have to buy something tomorrow, I can get some silver from you. Darling, I have something else to tell you: the young mistress was also so kind as to give me a bag of fruit. Why don't you see what kind of fruit it is?

(Dong Yong) It is just two dates![7] That young lady is treating us with contempt. I would count it as a gift if she had given us one or two pounds. Why did she give us only two?

(Weaving Maiden) You eat one, and I will eat one, so each of us will eat one of these two dates. (They eat the dates.) She also gave me a pear.[8]

(Dong Yong) Now that we are traveling today, that pear is great to quench our thirst.

(Weaving Maiden) But we will have to divide it.

(Dong Yong) I don't have a knife here with me to cut it up.

(Weaving Maiden) Let me divide it with my nails. That beats cutting it up with a knife.

(Dong Yong) That's wonderful!

(Weaving Maiden) She also gave me a fan.

(Dong Yong) That fan is quite useful to protect you against the sun.

(Weaving Maiden) You take it as a keepsake!

(Dong Yong) Now you are clearly talking nonsense! For instance, when a merchant is traveling and has a lover, she will gave him a keepsake, but you and I are one husband and one wife who will stay together for all eternity, so why mention a keepsake?

(Weaving Maiden) Darling, that is not what I meant! If you will be studying away from home and cannot come back for the night, so we cannot see each other in the morning and in the evening, then it will be as if I am by your side as soon as you look on this fan. Is that intention wrong?

---

[6] This phrase, "from the same ingot" (*yiding fenkai*), has the same pronunciation as "we definitely have to part" (*yiding fenkai*).

[7] "Dates" (*zaozi*) has the same pronunciation as "May you have a son soon" (*zao zi*).

[8] "Pear" (*li*) has the same pronunciation as "separation" (*li*).

(Dong Yong) If that's the case, I will take this fan.

(Weaving Maiden) What are those birds over there?

(Dong Yong) Those are mandarin ducks!

[To the same tune]

(Dong Yong)
The mandarin ducks are sporting on the waves,
Pair upon pair forming couples.

(Weaving Maiden) Will these mandarin ducks ever separate?

(Dong Yong) How could they separate?

(Weaving Maiden) Too bad they are now floating on this creek, but one still has to go off to the Heavenly River.

In case an orchid boat rows by and they separate in fright . . .

(Dong Yong) During the daytime they swim about in couples, and during the night they sleep with intertwined necks!

(Weaving Maiden) The female duck will have to go off.

(Dong Yong) Then the male duck will also go away!

(Weaving Maiden) The male duck will not go away.

(Dong Yong) If the male duck doesn't go, the female duck will also not go.

(Weaving Maiden) She will go off as soon as I point at her with my finger!

(Dong Yong) She definitely will not go away even if you hit her with a stone, let alone if you only point at her with your finger!

(Weaving Maiden) If I point at the female duck, she will definitely go away!

(Dong Yong) Let me point at that male duck to see whether he will also go away. He doesn't even go away now that I clap my hands!

(Weaving Maiden) That silly bird doesn't know how to fly.

One bird flies over the shallow stream;
The other flies to the Heavenly River.

(Dong Yong) Darling, how come one flies off to the Heavenly River?

(Weaving Maiden) The one that goes off to heaven is the female bird, and the one staying behind on the stream is the male bird.

(Dong Yong) These birds are called loyal birds: they walk in pairs and sleep in pairs; they are never separated!

(Weaving Maiden) That's what you believe?

> Despite a harmony as of heaven and earth,
> Husband and wife are basically birds in the same forest:
> When the final moment arrives, each goes his own way!

(Dong Yong) Darling, you are quite talkative today!

[To the earlier tune]

(Weaving Maiden)
It is not that I am so talkative,
It's because I secretly shed tears.

I have to go back to heaven.

(Dong Yong) Darling,

> You haven't finished discussing the affairs of this world,
> So why do you say you will go up to heaven?

[To the earlier tune]

(Weaving Maiden)
I'd like to tell you the whole story from the beginning,
And the words may well be on the tip of my tongue;
I still cannot bring myself to pronounce them—
Once I start telling, I'll feel a pain as if cut by knives!

[To the earlier tune]

(Dong Yong)
As husband and wife we live in close harmony,
So how could we be torn apart?
The proverb states: "Taking a wife is like cutting out an ax handle."[9]
My dear wife, please no more of that idle talk, those idle words.
There is no need for tears coursing down!

---

9   This line derives from a poem in the *Book of Odes*, which reads: "In hewing [the wood for] an ax handle, how do we proceed? / Without [another] axe it cannot be done. / In taking a wife, how do we proceed? / Without a go-between it cannot be done." Unintentionally Dong Yong draws attention to the irregular nature of their marriage.

(Weaving Maiden) I have to go off.

(Dong Yong) Where do you want to go to?

(Weaving Maiden) You go to your home, and I will go to my home.

(Dong Yong) Do you want to go to your natal home? Come to my house, and when we have worn mourning for three years for my mother, we will together go and visit your family, you riding a sedan and I riding a horse. That would make a good impression!

(Weaving Maiden) Where do you think my home is when you speak like this?

(Dong Yong) You are from Penglai Village.[10]

(Weaving Maiden) And where is your home?

(Dong Yong) In Dong Scholartree Village.

(Weaving Maiden) I am actually a moon princess from heaven, / But when the Jade Emperor learned about your filiality, / I was dispatched to the earth below to weave brocade. / For a full hundred days till my work was done—how could I refuse? My darling, if I hadn't been an immortal maiden, how could I have woven ten rolls of silk and brocade in one day and one night—and on top of that make one pair of shoes for you too? Just think about it!

(Dong Yong) But you promised me, I remember, that you'd be my wife/ When we met in the shade of the scholartree— / Now, when I count, exactly one hundred days ago!

[Wei fan xu]

(Dong Yong)
Why do you now all of a sudden talk about a separation?
You and I have been husband and wife for a hundred days.
Filled with a wonderful love and passion,
We shared both cushion and coverlet:
Where the husband led, the wife followed,[11]
So how can you now abandon me and leave me behind?
I had hoped, you know, that we would share a grave at the foot of
    Mt. Apricot Blossom
And had no idea that in the shade of the scholartree the two of us
    would separate!
Like a rustling rain the tears course down my cheeks;
Overcome by pain intertwined branches are torn apart.

---

[10]   Penglai is one of the floating islands of the immortals in the Eastern Ocean.

[11]   "The husband leads and the wife follows" is a description of a perfect marriage in traditional China.

(Together)
We go our separate ways,
Not knowing in what year and what month we will once again share
    the curtained bed.

[To the same tune]

(Weaving Maiden)
My dear husband, please listen to my explanation:
I am actually an immortal maiden from the palaces of the ninth heaven.
When the Jade Emperor noticed your filial piety and sincere intention,
He sent me down to the mortal world
To be your companion and your wife.
It's only because the term is fulfilled
That I must disregard our marriage vows
And cannot care about our wedded love.
It's not the case that I want to abandon you,
But I don't dare disobey the Jade Emperor's order!
To my dismay, intertwined branches are torn apart.

(Together)
We go our separate ways,
Not knowing in what year and what month we will once again share
    the curtained bed.

[To the same tune]

(Weaving Maiden)
He over there is Unsurpassable High Heaven,
While I on my side am dissolving into tears.
When he will return to his home,
He will have no father or mother,
Nor will he have a trusted wife!
I cannot stop these tears on my cheeks;
Truly, my innards are cut to pieces as small as an inch!

(Dong Yong) My dear wife, if you will truly ascend to heaven, please allow me
to express my gratitude with a bow.

I am filled with humble gratitude:
A debt of three years
Was paid off in less than a hundred days!
Filled with sadness at your disclosure,

Of course I am shedding tears without stop.
This silver I return to you—
Even if I had millions in gold,
I could not buy back my darling wife!
This hairpin I return to you—
Use it to bind up your hair,
Because it will not bind my darling wife!
This shoe cover and thread I return to you,
So it will not tie up my guts and my mind,
And I will not be saddened at the sight!
This fan I now return to you,
As on it is written:

> *The speckled bamboo flecked with gold suits an immortal princess:*
> *Her married love will not extend beyond a term of a hundred days.*
> *Once we have parted at Yang Pass,[12] we cannot meet again, because*
> *While I depart for the east, you will leave in a westerly direction.*

The fan is white as the snow,
It opens as a fully rounded moon.
And in that moon, one sees Chang'e,[13]
Who cannot stay with any mortal man.
I had truly hoped
That we would go home as husband and wife
And enjoy ourselves at the foot of Mt. Apricot Blossom,
But who would have known you'd abandon me halfway?
My dear wife, when you ascend to heaven,
You leave me behind in this world of dust,
With the result that I'll "long for the horse on seeing the saddle,"
Be saddened and pained on observing your objects,
With the result that my innards will be pulverized!

(Together)
We go our separate ways,
Not knowing in what year and what month we will once again share the
curtained bed.

---

12   Yang Pass (Yangguan) is mentioned in a widely popular parting poem by the poet Wang Wei (d. 761).

13   Chang'e is the goddess of the moon who leads an eternal life of loneliness ever since she stole her
husband's immortality medicine.

[To the same tune]

(Weaving Maiden)
I have something I have to tell you:
On no account should you be filled with grief, be obsessed with longing,
Abandon sleep, and forget to eat!
Because all in vain you would suffer from love-longing,
Without anyone around to mix your medicines for you.
Please remember what I have to say:
I have been pregnant for these last three months
But do not know whether it will be a boy or a girl.
If it is a boy,
I will report his birth to the heavenly officials and bring him to you;
If it happens to be a girl,
This will be the end of our married love,
As I'm afraid that Her Majesty will keep me in the lunar grottoes.[14]
Wounded by sadness,
I can only dissolve into tears;
As my innards are broken,
I stare on the clouds and the sun all in vain!

(Together)
We go our separate ways,
Not knowing in what year and what month we will once again share the curtained bed.

(Dong Yong) My dear wife, please come down!

(Weaving Maiden) My darling, don't cry and weep!

(Dong Yong) My dear wife, don't ascend to heaven. I will happily go down on my knees to beg you!

(Weaving Maiden) Kneeling down in front of me is of no use at all. You might do better by kneeling down in front of the scholartree.

(Dong Yong) And what would be the point of kneeling down in front of the scholartree?

(Weaving Maiden) I will tell you what to say! You say: "Dear scholartree, my matchmaker, as you spoke up in the beginning, you also have to speak up today. Today my wife wants to go up to heaven, so tell her on my behalf not to go up

---

14 "Her Majesty" refers to the Queen Mother of the West, the ruler over all female immortals.

to heaven." He only has to speak one word, and I will not go.

(Dong Yong) You will not go?

(Weaving Maiden) I will not go. You only have to hold me back.

(Dong Yong) Dear scholartree, my matchmaker, as you spoke up in the beginning, you also have to speak up today. Today my wife wants to go up to heaven, so tell her on my behalf not to go up to heaven. Why do you not say a single word in reaction?

[Coda]

At the foot of the scholartree I shout and shout again;
I shout till my throat is hoarse, but still no answer!
Even a man of iron or stone would be moved to tears!

(Weaving Maiden) My dear husband, don't cry and weep. I am not meant to be your wife; Miss Saijin is meant to be your wife. Among the ten rolls of colored brocade I wove at the Fu mansion, there is one roll of flying dragons and flying phoenixes. If you present that one roll to the court, your status and career will be ensured.

My dear husband, do not go on crying:
Miss Saijin is destined to be your wife.
As for another meeting with me, you'll run
Into a divine immortal on the capital's streets. (Exit)

[Zhuyunfei]

(Dong Yong)
My darling wife has gone away,
As far as I may look, she has disappeared!
My innards are shattered because of my weeping,
And I have lost my voice because of my shouting.
Oh, abandoning me, you ascend the staircase to heaven,
So I'm saddened and wounded by a bitter pain.
With my eyes wide open
I stare on the cloudy hills,
But nowhere see my darling wife.
She has discarded her silken dress,
So I'll never be able to see her again.
How I hate that scholartree for making this match,
How I hate that scholartree fr making this match! (Exit)

WEAVING BROCADE (*Zhijin ji*)

from The Comprehensive Catalog with Content Summaries of the Ocean of Song

This play is also known by the name of *The Heavenly Immortal* (*Tianxian ji*). According to the printed version it was composed by the actor Gu Jueyu. It tells of how Dong Yong of the Han dynasty sold himself out of filial piety and met with Weaving Maiden while on the road. It was named *Weaving Brocade* because Weaving Maiden weaves brocade to pay off his debt. The names of the characters and the details of the plot are mostly a fabrication. The play goes so far as to turn Dong Zhongshu into a son of Yong and a child of the heavenly immortal. It also states that Zhongshu's given name was Si. Dong Zhongshu lived under the Early Han and Dong Si lived under the Later Han,[15] many centuries apart from each other, but here they have been combined into one character! It also elaborates on how Yan Junping instructed Zhongshu on how to find his mother, how his mother was angered because Yan had divulged the secrets of heaven, and how she burned Yan's books on the changes and hexagrams and yin and yang. It is all too absurd for words!

[SUMMARY]

Dong Yong, whose style is Yanping, hails from Dong's Scholartree Village of Danyang County in Runzhou. His mother had died when he was young. His father had been a transportation commissioner but eventually had returned home and thereupon had also passed away. Because Dong Yong was too poor to provide him with a proper funeral, he went to sell himself to the prefectural magistrate Fu Hua as a bonded laborer. Hua was living in his home village in retirement. He loved to do good works and he pitied Yong because he was so filial, so he provided him with all he needed, whereupon Yong went back home with the money. Because of Yong's filial behavior, the Astral God of Great White[16] reported Yong to the Emperor Above, who ascertained that Seventh

---

[15]   Dong Si lived in the final decades of the second century C.E. and the first decades of the third century C.E.

[16]   Great White is the planet Venus. The Astral God of Great White often appears in traditional popular tales in the guise of an old man who comes to the aid of the tale's hero or heroine when he or she is in distress. The god may act on his own initiative, but often he has been dispatched by the Jade Emperor.

Sister, the Weaving Maiden, had a karmic affinity with Yong, so the Emperor Above ordered her to go down to the mortal world for a hundred days and help him pay back his debt. When Yong was on his way to Fu, he met with the immortal maiden in the shade of a scholartree. She lied to Yong by telling him that she had lost her husband and wanted to become his wife because she was destitute. Yong adamantly refused her offer, but the Star of Great White transformed himself into an old man who strongly urged Yong to comply with her request, and the Star of Great White also made the scholartree reply to Yong's question and act as their matchmaker, so Yong believed the match was heavenly ordained and they went to Fu as a couple.

The immortal maiden claimed that she could weave ten bolts of brocade in a single day and night. Fu did not believe her but gave her an extra supply of thread to try her out. Because all the immortal maidens helped her in weaving, the ten bolts of brocade were all finished by dawn, and their dazzling colors were greatly admired by Fu, and he treated Yong as a guest. Fu's daughter Saijin became the immortal maiden's best friend, but Fu's son was a mean knave who tried to seduce the immortal maiden, whereupon she slapped him in the face.

When the period of one hundred days was up, she and Yong took their leave of Fu. She told Yong to present the dragon-phoenix brocade she had woven to the court, telling him that this would make his career and fame. She also showed him the poem in the brocade, saying: "Your marriage with Fu's daughter will also originate in this." Thereupon she disappeared on a cloud. Yong informed Fu of what had happened, and Fu realized that this miracle was due to his filial piety, so he gave him his daughter as wife.

When Yong took the brocade to the imperial palace, he was elevated by edict to the rank of Top-of-the-List[17] for Presenting Treasure. When he paraded through the streets [of the capital], the immortal maiden handed him a son and immediately disappeared. Yong called his son Si and gave him the style Dongshu. When he grew up, he was exceptionally intelligent. Because on one occasion people made fun of him for having no mother, Si visited Yan Junping. Junping told him to go to Great White Mountain on the seventh night of the Seventh Month: "Wait till seven maidens pass, and the seventh person, who is dressed in yellow, is your mother!"

When he did as he had been told, he indeed met with his mother. She gave him three gourds, saying: "Two of these are for you and your father, and one

---

[17]   The person who had placed first in the palace examinations after having passed the metropolitan examinations was called "top-of-the-list" (*zhuangyuan*), because his name appeared first on the public list of those who had passed the examination. The top-of-the-list was allowed to parade through the capital for three days to celebrate his success. The Top-of-the-List for Presenting Treasure is an invention of the author.

is for Junping." When Si came home, he gave one gourd to Junping. Suddenly flames burst forth from the gourd and burned Junping's secret books on yin and yang. This was because he had angered her by divulging the secrets of heaven.

[The account of this tale in] the *Soushen ji* reads:

When Dong Yong's father died, he did not have the means to bury him, so he sold himself as a slave. His master knew that he was virtuous, and so let him go with millions of cash. When Yong had worn mourning for three years, he wished to go back to his master to fulfill his duties as a slave. On the road he met a woman, who said she wanted to be his wife, and the two of them went together. His master said to Yong: "I gave you the money!" Yong answered: "Thanks to your grace, my father's funeral could be completed. Even though I am of no worth, I still want to serve you diligently with all my strength in order to repay your favors." His master then asked: "What are the skills of your wife?" Yong said: "She is skilled at weaving." The master then said: "If that's the case, let her weave a hundred bolts of double-threaded silk for me." Thereupon Yong's wife set to weaving for his master, and in ten days the hundred bolts were done.

THE TALE OF THE SHADY SCHOLARTREE

Late-imperial China knew a rich culture of narrative traditions, each with its own performers and audiences, styles, topics, and occasions for performance. Some performers told their stories in prose, others in alternating prose and verse, and others in long ballads all in verse. Some performed in teahouses, small theaters, and other public venues, while others performed in private homes or only on specific ritual occasions.

The genre of "pulling songs"(wange) from the Hubei-Hunan area, which was also known by a variety of other names such as "funerary drumming" (sanggu) and "filial songs" (xiaoge), was performed at night during the days leading up to a funeral. Local styles and formats for the performance might show great differences, but as a general rule, a performance would be introduced by three rolls of the drum. After the performer had invited the gods to be present at the performance, he would first praise the deceased and then perform his main tale (zhengshu).[1] The tale of a filial son who is willing to sell himself into servitude may well have been considered a very suitable topic for such occasions. The performance would be concluded by sending off the gods.

A peculiar formal feature of the genre is that texts may be composed in stanzas of two rhyming seven-syllable lines, as is the case of The Tale of the Shady Scholartree. *The modern edition of the text is based on two printed editions from the final years of the Qing dynasty (1644–1911).[2] The plot of* The Tale of the Shady Scholartree *is much indebted to* Weaving Brocade. *The role of the evil son of Prime Minister Fu Hua, which most likely was originally created to provide a part for the clown/villain (chou) in a theatrical company, is much extended here. The character of Dong Yong's sworn brother Zhao Hei, whom we first encounter in* The Tale of the Shady Scholartree, *is probably also indebted to theatrical companies' need for a role for their martial star actor.*

---

[1] *Zhongguo quyi zhi. Hubei juan,* 1992, 117–9; *Zhongguo quyi zhi. Hunan juan,* 2000, 84–85.

[2] The following translation is based on the modern edition in Du, 1957, 57–69. That edition is collated on the basis of the late-Qing printed editions of the Wenyuantang of the Yao family of Toubao in Yiyang County in Hunan and of the Sanyuantang of the Huang family of Jiuzong in Zhongxiang, also in Hunan province.

ANONYMOUS

Printed from Newly Cut Blocks: The Tale of the Shady Scholartree—
How Dong Yong Practiced Filial Piety and Seventh Sister Descended to Earth, Part One

I will not sing of Heaven, and I will not sing of Earth,
But I will sing a story of a man who practiced filiality.

Listen to me sing the tale of Dong Yong's filial piety,
A filial piety that will even move an ironhearted man.

Dong Yong's home county is not all that far from here:
He hailed from Xiaogan County in Huangzhou Prefecture.

The place he lived was called Apricot Blossom Village,
And from the very beginning I will tell you all the details.

He was a student in the prefectural Confucian academy,
But because of years of famine, travail and trouble arrived.

The three years of dry spells and droughts were truly terrible;
His mother suffered such hunger she saw stars before her eyes.

His old mother of eighty was still alive at the time,
But he had no idea what to do and silently pondered.

So he thought of his mother's brother and his wife,
Who were living close by in a neighboring county.

Dong Yong therefore spoke as follows to his mother:
"I will go to my uncle's place and request a loan.

Whether I get some rice, or whether I get some silver,
Mother, I will borrow some so I can take care of you."

His mother instructed Dong Yong in the following words:
"Whether they have something for you or not, return quickly.

Whether it is something or nothing, come home swiftly
So your mother will not have to be worried about you."

After Dong Yong had taken his leave from his mother,
He went on his way as fast as his feet would carry him.

Of each ten steps he took traveling, nine were in a hurry,
And soon he had arrived in the township of his uncle.

After he had passed the main street and the small alleys,
He arrived at the house of his uncle, his mother's brother.

It happened that his uncle was not at home at the time;
His uncle's wife was in her room and spinning cotton.

She put aside the spinning wheel and greeted him, saying:
"Dong Yong, please don't insist on a formal greeting!"

She also asked her nephew the following question:
"What is the business that brings you to our house?"

Dong Yong answered her in the following words:
"I have come here to borrow some silver or rice.

After years of famine we have no provisions left:
Back home we have no rice; we have no firewood."

His aunt replied immediately in the following manner:
"We have no silver at all, and we certainly have no rice.

There is grain in the mill room but no one to pound it—
Do not come here and waste the time for your work."

Dong Yong knelt down on the earth on both his knees,
And he implored his aunt to help her relatives out.

His aunt made use of a trick to make herself scarce:
"I will go to my room and there get you some silver."

If you have to borrow, borrow from a noble man;
If you assist a person, assist him in his hour of need.

She quickly opened wide the door to her room—
Never again did he see her come out of her room.

Dong Yong only thought she was fetching something,
And he did not realize that his aunt was furious.

He waited for half a day, but she did not come out.
And so he had to go home with two empty hands.

Swallowing this insult, he could only go back;
He had not been able to borrow even half a penny!

His eyes were brimming with tears as he traveled on.
On the road he ran into his uncle, his mother's brother.

His uncle addressed him as follows: "Dear nephew,
What's the cause of your weeping so copiously today?"

Dong Yong replied to him in the following manner:
"Dear uncle, you have no idea of our bitter suffering!

After years of famine we have nothing left to eat,
So I went to your house to borrow something.

Who'd have thought that my aunt would be unkind?
She falsely feigned that she was going to her room."

His uncle cried: "Dong Yong, don't hate me for this!
Make haste to go home and take care of your mother.

When I get back home I will make my arrangements,
And I will have someone deliver some rice and silver."

When Dong Yong went on and arrived back home,
His eyes brimmed over with tears as he saw his mother.

His mother addressed the following question to him:
"My son, what is the cause that I hear you weeping?"

Dong Yong answered his mother in the following words:
"Dear mother, you have no idea how miserable I was!

It happened that my uncle, your brother, was not at home,
But my aunt, his wife, was in her room spinning cotton.

I explained all our sufferings to your brother's wife,
But all she had to say was only: 'We have nothing.'"

When the mother heard what her son had to tell her,
She immediately fainted and soon had passed away.

Her three souls disappeared,[1] her life off to the shades:
His dear mother's existence had turned into emptiness.

Think as he might, Dong Yong did not know what to do;
His eyes brimming over, his tears coursed down.

As he was weeping, he continued to think about it,
And he placed his mother's corpse in the high hall.

Dong Yong called for his sworn brother Zhao Hei:
"How do I get the money to buy my mother a coffin?"

In his desperation he also spoke to Zhao Hei as follows:
"I will sell my body to whoever is willing to buy me!

Dear brother, I want to discuss this matter with you—
I wouldn't mind selling my body to bury my mother!"

Zhao Hei answered Dong Yong in the following words:
"Dear brother, there is none who would want to buy you!

You are a student in the prefectural Confucian academy—
Why would you want to sell your body to buy a coffin?

Even if some rich guy would be willing to buy you,
He would have you carry firewood and haul water.

He would want you to hoe the fields and work at farming—
How would you be able to do that kind of hard labor?

Dear brother, you better devote yourself to your studies:
Since ancient times, the books have always been profitable.

And when one day the imperial list will be posted,
You will be awarded the title of 'top-of-the-list.'

You stay at home and take care of your mother,
But let me sell my body and buy her a coffin!"

Dong Yong immediately made clear to Zhao Hei:
"You sell your body? You're way too impulsive!

---

[1]   In traditional China a person was credited with three souls. After a person's death, according to one theory, one soul would take up residence in the ancestral tablet, one soul would stay with the corpse, and one soul would travel to the underworld to be judged.

Dear brother, if you indeed would sell your body,
My reputation would be greatly damaged by that.

In raising her son, she displayed such great love,
But her own children would not know gratitude!

You stay here and guard the corpse of my mother,
And I will go and sell my body to buy her a coffin!"

With a marker of straw on his body he walked the street,[2]
Calling out again and again: "I am selling my body!"

He walked from one end of the street to the other:
"Who in this world of famine is willing to buy me?"

He walked from the eastern end to the western end—
Dong Yong kept shouting, weeping in a piteous manner.

When he walked through Apricot Blossom Village,
He ran into a prime minister with the surname Fu.

His Excellency the Prime Minister questioned him:
"What is the cause that you want to sell your body?

You are a student in the prefectural Confucian school;
You have no reason to take your body onto the street!

How come you are not practicing essays in your study
But dare commit such a shameless and impudent act!

You dishonor us scholars and the great sage Confucius;
Your parents never should've brought you into this world!"

Dong Yong knelt down on the earth on both his knees:
"Your Excellency the Prime Minister, please listen to me.

I had a dear mother of eighty who was living with me,
But now she has died, and I am at a loss about what to do.

As I do not have a coffin in which I may bury her,
I can only offer my body for sale on the streets."

---

[2] A marker of straw advertises goods for sale.

The prime minister heard of Dong Yong's filiality:
"Such filial piety is rare in the whole wide world!

Seeing you want to sell your body to bury your mother,
Even an ironhearted, insensitive man would be moved.

Seeing that you, Dong Yong, practice filial piety,
I will weigh out the silver and give it to you.

I will give you ten ounces of snow-white pure silver,
And you will go home and then bury your mother.

I will ask for no interest on those ten ounces of silver,
But you will work as a laborer for me for three years.

You will come to my place and work there as a laborer;
When after three years your work is done, you go home."

Paper and brush, ink and inkstone were brought out
To write out a labor contract that might serve as proof.

So he immediately wrote out that single labor contract—
As Dong Yong raised the brush, his tears coursed down.

In his hand he raised the brush with its goat's-hair tip—
Before he had written one character, his tears fell down.

He raised the brush, and he wrote down his name:
"I have no coffin for my mother and so sell my body.

I am without son and I am also without daughter;
I am at present a single person who is his own master.

I am without wife, and I am also without neighbors;
My only connection is my sworn brother Zhao Hei."

When Dong Yong had finished writing the labor contract,
[Minister Fu said:] "I give you your ten ounces of silver.

Once you've buried your mother, come take up your job;
I will keep the labor contract here in my house."

As soon as Dong Yong had the silver in his hands,
He went home as fast as his feet would carry him.

Once he had the silver, he made the arrangements,
So he went to the main street to buy a good coffin.

After he had bought the wooden coffin trestles,
He placed his mother's coffin in the main hall.

He chose and selected a good day and lucky time
And buried her in her tomb, all according to rule.

Near the tomb they built a grave-guarding terrace,
And Dong Yong and Zhao Hei wept piteously.

Now today the yellow gold had sunk into the earth;
They had no worry in the world as they went home.

When Dong Yong came back home, he gathered his luggage,
And the two sworn brothers said good-bye to each other.

Zhao Hei decided he wanted to seek his luck elsewhere;
He peddled straw sandals walking up and down the street.

He asked for half a liter of rice for three pairs of sandals
And figured that that was not a good way to survive.

As Zhao Hei lay sleeping in the shade of a parasol tree,
An immortal maiden appeared in his dream and said:

"I give you this precious sword and book of strategy:
Make sure to memorize each line of it by heart!"

When Zhao Hei woke up again from his dream,
He then privately thought all alone to himself:

"Now I have this book of strategy and precious sword,
I will flaunt my heroism on White Bones Mountain!"[3]

When he came to the foot of White Bones Mountain,
Its five hundred bandits were truly quite fearsome.

They blocked the road and wanted his money, but
As soon as Zhao saw them, his rage rose to heaven!

Zhao Hei addressed them in the following words:
"A chicken egg cannot fight against lance and sword!

---

[3] White Bones Mountain is not an actual place-name. The name suggests a place where many men have lost their lives—apparently because they have been killed by the bandits who occupy the mountain.

Come over here quickly, surrender and submit to me,
And hand over all the money you took from travelers.

If you don't hand over the money you took from travelers,
None of you five hundred bandits will keep his life!"

The five hundred bandits laughed out loudly and said:
"This guy really has no idea what he's telling us!

He is a single person, all alone and without help,
Yet he demands the money we took from travelers!"

The two sides fell to fighting and fought a round,
And in that fight the bandits were utterly defeated.

The Great King of the Mountain,[4] at his wit's end,
Cried out to his bandits: "Let's all welcome him!

We invite you up our mountain to be our Great King;
You'll get all our silver and gold, jewels and treasure.

You will be the commander in chief on the mountain;
You will be in charge of us bandits without number!"

Once he was in charge of the many myriads of bandits,
Zhao Hei gave them the following virtuous orders:

"Do not kill young children and pitiable orphans;
Don't kill men and women who are in mourning.

Don't kill the aged and those who are all by themselves:
In these three major issues you have to do as I say!"

"These five hundred bandits are yours to order about;
This Great King of the Mountain surrenders to you!

Now you will be the Great King here on this mountain,
And you'll wear the golden armor that clings and clangs."

But let's not sing of Zhao Hei and of his good fortune;
Let me sing again of Dong Yong on his way to his job.

Having buried his mother, he left to take up his job;
His eyes brimming with tears, he walked on all alone.

---

4   A bandit leader often is designated as "great king."

But because Dong Yong displayed such filial piety,
His filiality even moved Heaven, even moved Earth!

Because the filial piety of Dong Yong was so sincere,
The Jade Emperor on High was informed of the cause.

The Jade Emperor on High gave out an order
To his seven daughters in the imperial palace

In which he instructed the seven sisters in the palace
To have one of them give up her place in the palace:

"On earth a certain Dong Yong practices filiality,
So We bestow on him an immortal maiden as wife.

One hundred days is set as the limit of this marriage;
After a hundred days, the marriage bond is dissolved.

When the hundred days are over, she returns to heaven,
And husband and wife each will go their separate ways."

The seven sisters got together to discuss this matter:
"Seventh Sister, you go down to the mortal world!

You will be the marriage partner of that Dong Yong;
When the hundred days are over, you'll return to heaven.

We will give you a magic treasure of orchid incense—
All you will have to do is just enjoy married life.

If you, Seventh Sister, are in danger, just burn this incense,
And we, your six sisters, will come down from heaven."

After Seventh Sister had received the orchid incense,
She traveled on a cloud to the world of mortal men.

Soon she arrived near a pond shaded by a scholartree:
"Mountain spirit and god of the earth, listen well!

Mountain spirit and god of the earth, these are my orders—
I am Seventh Sister, an immortal from the world above.

At the Jade Emperor's order I've descended to earth
To become the marriage partner of one Dong Yong.

You, mountain spirit, change into a three-room house,
And you, god of the earth, take position near the tree."

She instructed the god of the earth: "You act as my uncle,
And the shady scholartree will act as the matchmaker."

Then the immortal maiden sat down beneath the tree,
And immediately she saw Dong Yong passing by her.

As he was standing in the road he thought to himself:
"How come there is such a bench beneath the tree?"

Dong Yong thought silently to himself in his heart:
"The breeze beneath the tree we will share together."

He quickly took a few steps as he walked in a hurry
And also sat down to rest in the tree's cool shade.

The immortal maiden immediately cried out: "Uncle!
Dear uncle, god of the earth, hurry up and come here."

The immortal maiden addressed her uncle as follows:
"Dear uncle, there is something I have to tell you.

Fortunately this Dong Yong is a single young man;
Still, he should keep his hands off your niece's body."

Dong Yong then addressed her uncle as follows:
"Dear uncle, allow me to give you an explanation!

Because my mother died and I couldn't buy a coffin,
I sold my body in bondage to that Prime Minister Fu.

I've just buried my mother, not yet started my job,
And I just sat down here to rest awhile in the shade.

But suddenly your niece pressed herself against me—
Uncle, please don't blame me, this unmarried man!"

When her uncle had heard these words of Dong Yong,
[He said:] "Such filial piety is hard to find in this world!

Even a man with guts of iron or stone would be grieved—
Only by selling your body could you bury your mother.

As I see that you indeed practice such filial piety,
I will give you my niece as your marriage partner.

Because your filial piety is indeed so true in nature,
I want the two of you to tie the knot here on the spot."

Dong Yong answered him in the following words:
"Where is the lamb and pork, and where is the wine?

We are also without a dress, without gold and silver:
I really, really would not dare tie the wedding knot."

Her uncle then spoke to him in the following words:
"Even without pork and wine it can still be done.

There's no need of gold and silver or a wedding dress;
All put together, I'll have you be husband and wife."

Dong Yong then asked the girl the following question:
"But then, there is here no matchmaker or witness?"

The girl answered him in the following manner:
"Young man, what you say now is not very smart.

In ancient times Meng Jiangnü from Fengzhou
Searched for a husband by grabbing a willow.[5]

My uncle will serve as the man who gives me away,
And as matchmaker will serve the shady scholartree."

Dong Yong thereupon called out to the shady scholartree.
Laughing out loudly, he called out: "Shady Scholartree!"

"You called out three times; it responded three times:
As our matchmaker serves the shady scholartree!"

First they bowed to Heaven; next they bowed to Earth.
Thirdly they bowed to her uncle for fixing the marriage.

Fourthly they bowed to their matchmaker, the scholartree,
And inserting a straw in the road, they tied the wedding knot.[6]

---

[5] According to legend, the maiden Meng Jiang (Meng Jiangnü) takes the initiative in finding a husband without waiting for her parents' arrangements. When she is taking a bath in the pond behind her house, she notices she is being observed by a man hidden in a tree. She calls him down and insists on marrying him, as a woman's body can only be seen by her husband. She then takes him to see her parents, and the marriage is formally consummated. It turns out that her husband is a conscript laborer who had fled the hardships of building the Great Wall. When her husband returns to the construction site, he soon dies and is buried in the Great Wall. Meng Jiang then goes to find him and brings down the Great Wall by her weeping. See Idema, 2008.

[6] This line is unclear to me.

Now husband and wife today had performed the rites,
And Dong Yong addressed her in the following words:

"I have sold my body in bondage to be a laborer,
So where will you, my dear wife, go find a home?"

The young bride in her turn replied to her husband:
"'Marry a man and follow that man wherever he goes.'

Now that I have married you, I will go wherever you go.
Husband and wife are like water; they can't be apart."

When Dong Yong heard this, he was filled with joy;
Husband and wife continued their journey to Mr. Fu.

They took their leave of her uncle and the scholartree;
Holding hands, husband and wife went on their way.

Husband and wife, a couple, a pair, went as workers,
And so they arrived together at the house of Mr. Fu.

The squire immediately asked what had happened:
"How is it possible that today there are two of you?

Originally you said that you had no relatives or kin.
On the contract it states that you are a single man.

How come you now show up with a lovely bride?
It cannot be that you kidnapped her while traveling?

Quickly tell me the truth about where she is from;
Otherwise I will send you off to the county office.

That's the way to escape their judicial torture—
Tell me what happened, from the very beginning!"

Dong Yong knelt down on the earth on both his knees,
And he gave the squire a straightforward account:

"After the day I had finally buried my mother,
My sworn brother and I went our separate ways.

When I on my way here passed by a scholartree,
A young girl was sitting beneath it in its shade.

The scholartree was growing by the side of the road,
So I also decided to rest for a while in its cool shade.

Then her elderly uncle walked over to us, and he
Wanted his niece to tie the marriage knot with me.

He was her uncle, the man to give the bride away,
And the shady scholartree acted as our matchmaker.

Her uncle told me to call out to the scholartree to see
Whether the tree was willing to serve as matchmaker.

When I called out three times, it replied three times;
The tree spoke and confirmed it was our matchmaker."

The squire was immediately willing to trust his story,
So he also secretly questioned the young woman:

"What is the name of your father and mother?
Where are you from? From which county and village?"

The young woman answered him as follows:
"I used to live beyond the clouds of the highest skies.

My father has no surname, my mother has no name,
And I roamed at leisure through the halls of heaven."

"As you have come here together with your husband,
What work can you do? Can you cook? Can you sew?"

The young woman addressed him in the following words:
"I sculpt and embroider flowers of a hundred kinds.

I artfully weave patterned silks in thousands of styles.
Give me ten pounds of thread, and I'm done in one night.

Even if you would give me ten pounds of yellow thread,
In a single night I would weave it all into patterned silk!"

When the squire heard this, he was filled with joy;
He ordered a serving maid to weigh out the thread.

"Ten pounds of yellow thread will go to your room.
By dawn tomorrow it must be woven into a pattern."

Dong Yong immediately started to curse his wife:
"Why did you have to boast about your abilities?

No one, I fear, can weave that much in a single night—
In this way we will never be able to leave the Fus!"

The young woman answered her husband as follows:
"Have the courage to relax, and just take your rest.

My husband, there's no need for you to worry at all,
And in a single night I will finish all the weaving."

The young woman waited until her husband slept,
Then burned her orchid incense in a golden burner.

As soon as one stick of orchid incense was burned,
Her six sisters, each and every one, had all arrived.

"When we smelled that you burned the incense,
The six of us together descended from heaven."

Seventh Sister addressed them in the following manner:
"I have asked you to come to weave floral silks."

The seven sisters—of one mind, united in purpose—
Set up the loom, threw the shuttle, weaving a piece.

Five of them threw the shuttle, two of them pulled,
And two of them lifted the thread, pushing the swing.

Their silk displayed the patterns of heaven and earth;
Their silk displayed the empire's mountains and rivers.

Their silk displayed the major stars and lesser stars;
Their silk displayed the sun and moon blazing in the sky.

Their silk displayed the palace halls of highest heaven;
Their silk displayed the Jade Emperor holding court.

Their silk displayed the Eight Immortals gathered together,
The Eight Immortals drinking wine at a feast in heaven.

Their silk displayed Guanyin and Lü Dongbin
As these two met each other on Luoyang Bridge.[7]

---

[7]   The Luoyang Bridge referred to here is the Luoyang Bridge of Chaozhou with its seventy-two arches, built by the divine craftsman Lu Ban. When the money had run out and the project was not yet completed, the bodhisattva Guanyin appeared in a boat close to shore and seduced all the men of the place to fill it with gold and silver. Lü Dongbin is one of the most popular characters of the Eight Immortals.

Their silk displayed ocean dragons and sea horses;
Their silk displayed two dragons playing with a pearl.

Their silk displayed civil officials and military officers;
Their silk displayed the princes and prime ministers.

Their silk displayed phoenixes true to color;
Their silk displayed a running herd of unicorns.

Their silk displayed carp jumping across the Dragon Gate;[8]
Their silk displayed mandarin ducks in their blazing colors.

Their silk displayed a gibbon monkey stealing fruits,
A hare watching the moon,[9] an arrow hitting the target.

Their silk displayed a deer holding flowers in its mouth,
Together with lucky magpies and with black ravens.

Their silk displayed a male swan and a white crane,
And the Golden Rooster announcing dawn without fail.

They continued weaving till the cock announced dawn
And they had finished weaving all their patterned silks.

When they'd used up the ten pounds of thread,
The red sun had not yet risen in the eastern sky.

So she also made a pair of shoes for Dong Yong,
And only then the red sun appeared in the sky.

The floral silks they had woven were truly lovely,
And her six sisters returned to their heavenly realm.

Once her six sisters had entered the heavenly palace,
She took and held the floral silks in her hands.

When Don Yong saw how beautiful these silks were,
He shook his head in amazement, scared out of his wits:

"What you've produced is absolutely fabulous!
My wife, your actions live up to your words!"

---

[8] By jumping across the Dragon Gate rapids in the Yellow River, carp were said to turn themselves
into dragons.

[9] The moon is inhabited by a hare that is continuously employed in preparing the elixir of immortality.

And when the eastern sky was clear and bright,
He took these silks to the squire in his high hall.

At the first sight of these floral silks the squire
Also said: "The work she did is truly marvelous!"

The depicted dragons and phoenixes were out of the ordinary,
So he ordered [his daughter] Saijin to store the silks in a chest.

The squire also told his son so he would understand:
"On no account you can treat Dong Yong too lowly!

Don't treat student Dong as a lowly person—his wife
Is a heavenly immortal who has descended to earth."

He also said to Dong Yong: "Go study your books!
Your wife embroiders flowers in the embroidery room.

Let her weave her floral silks with my little daughter
And, in the embroidery room, engage in needlework.

The two of them are of one mind, united in purpose;
They work together in harmony just like two sisters."

But let's not sing of how Saijin learned her feminine skills—
I will sing of the devious plot of the son of the squire!

Printed from Newly Cut Blocks: The Tale of the Shady Scholartree—
How Dong Yong Practiced Filial Piety and Seventh Sister Descended to Earth, Part Two

When he saw how beautiful that young woman was,
He conceived of a scheme of the most horrible nature.

He was determined to cause the death of student Dong,
Because he wanted to tie the knot with his lovely wife.

He said to Dong Yong: "Now you listen to my orders.
I want you to go and cut down a flowering pear tree.

Go and cut the wood on White Bones Mountain;
Cut down a pear tree there and then bring it here.

It has to be a pear tree, that is for sure,
So remember that well and don't mess it up.

I will hire a carpenter to make a bed out of it, because
When fall is cool, in the Eighth Month, I'll get a wife."

When Dong Yong had heard this order, [he thought:]
"This is the worst disaster that could happen to me!

White Bones Mountain is infested by bandits,
So I fear that I will not return with my life."

He went to his room and he called out his wife;
The two of them discussed how to deal with this.

As his tears coursed down, he told his wife:
"The young master ordered me to cut a pear tree,

But that mountain there is infested by bandits,
So I fear that I will not return with my life."

The young woman spoke to her husband as follows:
"Have the courage to relax: just go and do it.

My husband, you do not have to be worried;
I will take care of any danger on the mountain!"

After these words Dong Yong set out on the road:
Each step forward was followed by one step back.

The very first day after Dong Yong had left,
The young master tried to seduce his wife.

Oh-so-lightly he walked to the embroidery room;
In a soft voice he called out to her in a whisper.

The young woman immediately rose to her feet.
She took him for her husband who had returned.

But as soon as she saw it was young master Fu,
She was immediately startled out of her mind.

The young master entered the embroidery room
And promptly raised the subject of "happy joy."[10]

"You are truly smart in embroidering flowers;
I have come here because of our common joy."

He went on by bowing slightly before the woman:
"I'm here to ask for the game of fish and water.[11]

I am the eldest son in the house of squire Fu;
My red cassia tree in the moon lacks a Chang'e.[12]

I have stolen some time to come to this place,
Trying to catch the ocean dragon with a hook of gold.

I will give you, young woman, an ingot of gold;
Please take pity on me, as I am a single person.

Leave this embroidery room—don't crave the needle—
But come and have some fun with me for a while!

Let me tell you, young woman, don't be upset—
Which rose-cheeked girl doesn't love a rake?"

---

10 "Happy joy" is a common euphemism for sex.

11 "Fish and water" is a common image for lovemaking.

12 The cassia tree is one of the fixtures of the moon in Chinese folklore. The moon is inhabited by the beautiful goddess Chang'e, who fled to the moon after stealing and swallowing her husband's immortality medicine. As a result, she condemned herself to an eternity of loneliness and love-longing.

Dong Yong's wife answered him as follows:
"Sir, the words you just spoke lack common sense.

Riches and glory are determined from birth by fate—
How could I out of love for riches despise poverty?

Hurry up and make haste to go back to your place;
Don't you dare try to seduce me with your glib talk.

On no account will I give in to what you want,
You shameless and impudent beastly character!

I am by birth a virtuous woman of a decent family—
How could I, the same woman, mate with two men?"

Dong Yong's wife paid him no attention at all
But silently recited a spell that called down thunder.

She raised the thunder gods of the five directions,
The Lord of Thunder in a flash of light struck with fire!

Only a single flash of lightning and thunder strike—
Young master Fu had almost lost his life and died!

In a sudden instant the roaring thunder rumbled
And with a crashing sound hit young master Fu!

It burned away his eyebrows, burned away his beard—
The young master had almost lost his life for fright!

Because he had been burned black in this encounter,
He panicked and fled, and he made himself scarce.

"How could I know the Lord of Thunder would hit me?
Today I've no face to meet the elders east of the river.[13]

---

[13] Upon the death of the First Emperor of the Qin in 210 B.C.E., rebellions broke out all over China. One of the most successful leaders of the revolt was Xiang Yu, who had set out from the region "east of the River" (the Jiangnan region) with three thousand young men. The highborn Xiang Yu was a formidable fighter who was never defeated in battle, but he eventually lost out in the struggle for supreme power to the lowborn and cowardly Liu Bang, who knew to surround himself with able advisers and generals. When Xiang Yu had lost all his troops in 202 B.C.E., a fisherman offered to ferry him across the River so he could raise new soldiers, but Xiang Yu refused as he could not face the parents of the young men he had led into battle (Sima, 1959, 336). In a final confrontation with the troops of Liu Bang, he later committed suicide.

But it's only High Heaven than can annihilate me—
He struck me so hard I almost burst into fire!"

Young master Fu also said the following words:
"I am almost sure she must be an immortal maiden.

Because if she is not a divine immortal maiden,
How could she call down the thunder and rain?"

Let's not sing of the young man's attempt at seduction;
Let's sing again of Dong Yong: he left for the mountain.

With every step he took he wept for a while—
But August Heaven will not fail a filial person!

When he arrived at the foot of White Bones Mountain,
The mountain was indeed covered with fine pear trees.

Dong Yong was the only one reckless enough
To lower his head and to cut down a pear tree.

But before he had cut down even a single tree,
He was arrested by hundreds of bandits.

"Arrest him and lead him before the Great King!
How do you dare damage our mountain groves?

All the ten thousand things of the world have an owner—
You refuse to walk the road that leads to heaven's gate

But want to enter into hell even though it has no gate."
When the Great King learned of this, he was not amused,

And he promptly set about questioning Dong Yong:
"Where are you from? From which township, which county?

What is your surname and name, and where do you live?
Tell me everything from the start, without any lie!"

Dong Yong knelt down on the ground on both his knees:
[Said:] "Your Majesty, please listen to my explanation.

I hail from Xiaogan Township in Huangzhou County,
And I originally lived in Apricot Blossom Village.

But because I had not a coffin when my mother died,
I sold my body in bondage to the Fu-family mansion.

Having obtained the silver, I buried my mother—
Alas, for all the bitter sufferings I had to endure!

I have one sworn brother by the name of Zhao Hei.
In Apricot Blossom Village we had to say good-bye.

And ever since, I have been separated from him;
My heart has always been filled with longing for him."

When Zhao Hei realized this was his younger brother,
He hurried to pull him to his feet with both his hands.

He pulled his brother to his feet, and tears flowed down;
The two of them each told what had happened to him.

Zhao Hei asked his brother the following question:
"How is it possible that you look so emaciated?"

"It is because the young master wanted a pear tree.
I did not come to this mountain by my own mistake!

If Your Majesty had not turned out to be my brother,
I most likely would have lost my life, never to return!"

The two of them drank some wine and talked in confidence.
"For what reason have you ended up as their Great King?"

Zhao Hei told Dong Yong thereupon as follows:
"This place is not an area where one should come.

When earlier I reached White Bones Mountain,
The robbers kept me and did not allow me to return.

They wanted me to be the Great King of the Mountain;
Their gold and silver, jewels and treasure were mine.

I became the commander in chief on this mountain;
I am in charge of all the bandits, too many to count.

All those who are robbers now live in fear of me;
The five hundred bandits have all submitted to me.

Each day I take my pleasure here on the mountain;
All of a sudden already some months have passed.

I now will summon those five hundred bandits!"
Those five hundred bandits all promptly arrived.

"You five hundred bandits, listen to my orders!
Everyone will deliver a pear tree for this man.

Each of you will deliver for him a single tree,
And they will all be delivered to the Fu mansion."

The Great King also ordered the bandits as follows:
"When you meet with the squire, tell him loudly and clearly:

'Why did you want him to go and cut some wood?
He almost lost his life, would not have come back!'"

Zhao Hei also spoke to his brother as follows:
"Don't be concerned when you go back to the Fus.

Here are ten ingots of gold and ten ingots of silver;
I give them to you as a present as you go back."

When Dong Yong arrived back home again,
His tears flowed down when he saw his wife.

As soon as the squire saw this, he asked the reason,
Calling out time and again: "Dear Mr. Dong,

What kind of business took you out of the house?
I here at home did not know about it at all!"

Saijin spoke to her father in the following manner:
"My elder brother wanted him to cut a pear tree,

So he went to White Bones Mountain to cut the wood,
And he cut down the pear tree that he brought home."

As soon as the squire had heard the words of his daughter,
He immediately cursed his son: "You rotten scoundrel,

That Great King is definitely not your sworn brother.
How would you have been able to come back alive?"

The squire then spoke to Dong Yong as follows:
"A hundred days have passed, three full months.

You, husband and wife, listen to what I have to say.
Ready your luggage, the two of you, and go home.

I will give you ten ounces of the purest white silver—
Take it with you back home as a means of support.

Once you have some silver and have settled down,
You, husband and wife, will still have to make a living."

Upon these words Dong Yong replied as follows:
"My three years of labor have not yet come to an end.

On top of that you have the kindness to give us silver.
How will I be able to pay you back for all these favors?"

The squire in his high hall spoke as follows:
"I'll take the floral silk in payment for your debt."

Husband and wife came forward and made four bows:
"Please accept our thanks for your great kindness!

We are the beneficiaries of your exceeding kindness.
On what day will we ever be able to pay you back?"

[Saijin said to Seventh Sister:]

"First I give you, young woman, a packet of dates:
Take them with you on your trip as something to eat.

Secondly I give you, young woman, a fine snow pear:
On the road it will stop your thirst and still your hunger.

Thirdly I give you, young woman, a scarf and a fan:
Take them home with you as a memory and souvenir.

Fourthly I give you, young woman, a pair of shoes,
Which I made you myself with my very own hands."

Husband and wife accepted the gifts and went home,
But they found it hard to leave and tears flowed down.

After they had left the gate of the mansion of the Fus,
The two of them on the road were filled with gloom.

The immortal maiden realized the hundred days were up;
Feigning it was because of her small feet, she walked slowly.

For every step she took, she stopped and looked around,
Calling out time and again to her partner: "Please wait!"

As he urged her on and she tarried, they journeyed on
And eventually reached once more the shady scholartree.

Once there, they sat down in the shade of the tree,
And husband and wife, a couple, a pair, took a rest.

"I'm afraid this is the place where we'll have to part!"
And from her bosom she pulled out the packet of dates.

Husband and wife opened the packet, shared the dates,
And the two of them both were overcome by weeping.

With both her hands she pulled out the fan,
And she gave it to her husband as a souvenir.

Overcome by emotions she pulled out the pear,
With one slice of the knife cut it into two halves.

She also gave her husband a pair of shoes, [saying:]
"These I have made for you with my own hands."

When her husband heard this, he was not amused:
"Why do you start to say all this foolish nonsense?

I'd hoped that we would together live to old age,
So what is the reason that today we should part?

We've barely been husband and wife for three months,
So how can we all of a sudden go our separate ways?

'A single bamboo pole is beaten to its very end':
My dear wife, your words make no sense at all."

The young woman spoke to her husband as follows:
"Just look at that couple of birds resting by the pond.

The female bird flies off and soars up to heaven,
Leaving the male bird behind by the side of the pond."

Dong Yong replied promptly in the following words:
"When the magpies are flying, they fly as a couple.

Where the female bird goes, the male bird follows—
How could the male bird be willing to leave her?"

But as soon as he had finished speaking these words,
They indeed saw that female bird fly off and away.

So the female bird indeed had flown off and away,
And the young woman told him the reason and cause:

"The Jade Emperor noticed your exceptional filiality
And sent me down to the mortal world as your spouse.

He set a limit of one hundred days for our married life:
After these one hundred days I was to return to heaven.

The Jade Emperor summons me to the heavenly palace,
So today we are torn apart, separated from each other."

Dong Yong held on to his immortal bride while weeping:
"How can I let go of you so you can return to heaven?"

He held on to his immortal wife and wept till heartbroken:
"How can I let go of you to return to heaven's palace?"

But she cried out: "My husband, do not cry and weep,
But once again make a double bow before the scholartree.

If you can make the scholartree reply to your entreaties,
The two of us, husband and wife, will continue our marriage."

So Dong Yong again called out to the shady scholartree.
Despite his thousands of calls, there was no reaction at all.

He called till his throat grew hoarse and he lost his voice:
"How can you as a matchmaker suddenly have grown mute?"

The young woman devised a scheme to make herself scarce:
"Now you have to go and apologize to the scholartree!"

She tricked Dong Yong into weeping till he lost his mind:
"When I look around, my immortal bride has disappeared!"

An auspicious cloud carried her up to heaven,
And from her cloud she pronounced true words.

Dong Yong knelt down, weeping piteously:
"Please, immortal maiden, descend to earth!

I hope that you, my immortal bride, will descend to earth
To be united with me in marriage as we were before."

His immortal bride stood on her cloud and spoke:
"My dear husband, on no account keep longing for me!

Only if heaven collapses and the earth keels over
Will I be united in marriage with you once again.

But I have a few true words to tell you, my husband:
I am now already in the third month of pregnancy.

If the baby I will give birth to is a girl,
I will keep her with me in the palace of the moon.

But if the child I give birth to is a baby boy,
I will have him delivered to your home."

She also called: "My husband, do not be upset;
You will have another charming wife as before.

Demoiselle Saijin will be your wedded wife—
Why do you have to weep as if out of your mind?

Now that I have given you my instructions on all matters,
I will rush off on my rising cloud to heaven's palace."

Now that his immortal wife had left him to return to heaven,
Dong Yong returned to his home village while weeping.

Weeping all along the road, he arrived at the Fus.
As soon as the squire saw him, he asked the reason:

"You arrived as a couple, and you left as a couple,
So what is the cause that today you are awash in tears?

The two of you, husband and wife, departed together,
So what is the reason that you return all by yourself?"

Dong Yong promptly answered the squire as follows:
"Dear sir, I'll explain it to you so you may understand.

The wife that came here with me was an immortal maiden,
And below the shady scholartree she ascended to heaven."

When the squire heard these words, [he replied as follows:]
"Indeed she must have been a divine immortal maiden!

Because if she would not have been a divine immortal,
She'd not have finished those floral silks in a single night!"

The squire thereupon called out Saijin and ordered her:
"Bring me those floral silks so I can have a look!"

Demoiselle Saijin promptly opened the chest,
And from the chest a dazzling light shone forth.

When the floral silks were spread out before the hall,
All kinds of scenes were displayed in front of the hall.

A hundred kinds of immortal maidens appeared:
This kind of weaving was indeed out of the ordinary!

The squire at this sight conceived the following thought:
"I cannot keep these goods stored in my private home!

Wouldn't it be best to offer them up to the present ruler?
In that case Dong Yong is bound to achieve great fame."

He ordered Saijin to pack up these silks with great care,
And all together they traveled the road to the capital.

Hastily he took out and displayed this treasure,
All of a sudden in front of the golden steps.

He presented himself before the imperial throne, and
When his lord and king saw him, he asked him why.

The prime minister knelt down on the golden steps:
"Allow me to report this pleasant news to my ruler!

In Apricot Blossom Village in Xiaogan County
Happens to live a certain Dong Yong, a student.

Because when his mother died he had no coffin,
He sold his body in bondage to me, your minister.

When he came to my house to work off his debt,
Heaven sent down an immortal maiden as his spouse.

This immortal maiden could weave brocade silks,
Which were taken to me and displayed before the hall:

A hundred kinds of scenes displayed a dazzling light!"
He opened the chest and showed the silks to his king.

Depicted were tigers and phoenixes, with mandarin ducks;
The Eight Immortals were drinking wine, laughing loudly.

The emperor was filled with joy at this sight
And hastily summoned Dong Yong to court.

Dong Yong knelt down in the golden palace, and
The emperor granted him the rank of top-of-the-list.

He appointed him as top-of-the-list, the number one:
He was surrounded by the music of fifes and drums!

Escorted by runners in front and behind, on both sides,
He paraded through the streets of the city on horseback.

The top-of-the-list rode on horseback through the city,
And the prime minister gave him his daughter as bride.

Once demoiselle Saijin had become his wedded wife,
The whole family, old and young, shared in his glory.

Let's not sing of the marriage of the top-of-the-list;
Hear me sing of how the immortal maiden brought his son.

Bringing her baby, the maiden descended from heaven;
In the imperial city she waited for her man and master.

Standing on a bridge, she waited for her man to pass by
As he was parading through town, seated on his horse.

"Now the top-of-the-list is passing by this place,
I will block his way and not allow him to cross."

The top-of-the-list gave orders to find out the cause,
And all his runners cried out: "It's a female sprite!"

From her cloud the immortal maiden cursed her husband:
"How can you be so reckless, my man, as not to dismount?"

Repeatedly, time and again, she called out: "My husband!
I am not some dangerous female sprite, not at all!

If you now wear the black hat of office and carry a seal,
It's because of the floral silks you've offered to the court.

If the floral silks that I produced had not been so fine,
How could you have obtained the rank of top-of-the-list?

When I took my leave below the shady scholartree,
I told you I was already three months pregnant.

At that time, beneath the scholartree I made a promise
That I would bring you the child if it was a boy.

Yesterday I gave birth, and it is a baby boy,
So I have traveled on my cloud to this mortal world

With the purpose of bringing this baby boy to you."
When Dong Yong saw his wife standing on her cloud,

He hastily dismounted and knelt down on the ground:
"How could I have known this without your explanation?

How could I dare not accept your love and trust?
But I hope that you, my wife, will descend to earth.

Yes, I hope that you, my wife, will descend to earth
To be united with me in marriage as you were before."

His immortal wife stood on her cloud as she explained:
"My dear husband, don't foster such foolish thoughts!

From this day on I will be gone for good,
So I implore you, don't continue to be upset.

Take good care of my little baby boy;
Make sure he is free from trouble and pain.

Even though my son is still only little,
Don't treat my little boy like shit or straw,

Because, a few days after he comes down from heaven,
No one will remember anymore he is a divine immortal."

His immortal wife insisted on entering the gate of heaven;
Dong Yong, cradling the boy, sent her off with four bows.

He brought the boy with him to the house of the Fus,
And Saijin took the baby from him with a smile.

He thereupon instructed his wife as follows:
"Do not treat this baby boy lightly or lowly.

Even though he is still only very small,
This heavenly bestowed boy is truly great.

With his slender ten fingers and long arms,
He's bound to be a student when he grows up.

Let us bow to Heaven and Earth and the immortal maiden,
Praying for their protection of this boy so he may live long.

In his first and second years may he pass all dangers;
In his third and fourth years may he easily grow up.

In his fifth and sixth years may he enter school;
In his seventh and eighth years may he learn to read.

In his ninth and tenth years may he advance in his studies;
In his eleventh and twelfth years may he pass the exams.

May this immortal lad, bestowed today on us by Heaven,
Become a sturdy pillar of the state in the imperial court!"

One day turned into three, and three turned into nine,
And so he grew up into a man—a really handsome one!

His father and mother sent him to school, and
He showed exceptional talents in his studies.

The name he got in school was Dong Zhongshu—
In the mornings he recited his texts; at night he read.

But because he was with other boys at school,
They all cursed him as a child without mother:

"You may have a father, but you don't have a mother.
How do you dare share the same schoolroom with us?"

When Zhongshu heard this, he said not a word,
But once back home he asked: "Who's my mother?"

His father and mother refused to answer his question,
So he asked a fortune-teller to solve this riddle.

"Sit down on the bridge on the seventh of the Seventh,
And seven immortal maidens will cross the bridge.

The one who comes last, in a bright red skirt,
That one, the seventh, she is your mother!"

Soon it was already the seventh of the Seventh;
Zhongshu stood on the bridge as he had been told.

When he had waited on the bridge for quite some time,
Seven women appeared who wanted to cross the bridge.

The seventh woman indeed wore a bright red skirt, so
He grabbed her with both his hands, calling out: "Mother!"

The immortal maiden addressed him as follows:
"Who is the man who informed you of this?

I here am not your mother at all,
So please hurry up and go home.

But I will hand you this pair of gourds; please
Make sure to give them to Master Ghost-Valley.[14]

While on your way there, don't open them!
Make sure you remember that very well!

In case the master happens to be asleep,
Throw them on the roof and run away!"

---

[14] Master Ghost-Valley (or the Master of Ghost Valley; Guiguzi) is said to have lived during the period of the Warring States (fourth and third centuries B.C.E.). He was the teacher of the famous military strategists Sun Bin and Pang Juan. Later legend credited him with supernatural knowledge.

When Zhongshu heard this, he promptly left;
Every two steps he did in one single large step.

Quickly he threw the gourds on the roof:
The house was promptly burned to ashes.

The divination books were covered by an inkstone,
But even so, only a fragment was left for posterity.

Zhongshu immediately went back to the bridge.
From afar he saw the immortal maiden was still close by.

But when he had arrived back again at the bridge,
All he found was the bridge because his mother was gone.

All Zhongshu could do was to go back home
And to sit down again by the window in school.

Now, because he was originally of immortal descent,
The emperor granted him the rank of top-of-the-list.

He appointed him as top-of-the-list, the number one;
His whole family, old and young, shared in this boon.

The facts of Dong Yong's filial piety are really true;
They are transmitted in this world to his eternal fame.

APPENDIX

Weaving Maiden and Buffalo Boy in Myth and Fairy Tale

I

CLASSIC ACCOUNTS &
NOVELISTIC ADAPTATIONS

Weaving Maiden and Buffalo Boy are already mentioned in the ancient *Book of Odes*, which does not describe these stars as lovers but as slackers: despite her name, Weaving Maiden never finishes a single piece of cloth, and despite his name, Buffalo Boy and his animal never transport any cargo. In later legends they are lovers who are separated by the Heavenly River (the Milky Way). One of the texts in the second- or third-century *Nineteen Old Poems* (*Gushi shijiu shou*) describes their limitless longing as follows:

> Oh far so far, the star that leads the cow!
> Oh bright so bright, the maiden at the river!
> Oh slender so slender are her white hands,
> As click-clack she works loom and shuttle.
>   All day long she does not finish one pattern,
> The tears she cries pour down just like a rain.
> The Heavenly River is so pure and shallow,
> How far are they separated from each other?
>   Oh full so full—blocked by a single stream:
> Staring and gazing, but not allowed to speak![1]

By the beginning of the first millennium it was widely believed that these thwarted lovers were allowed to meet once a year, on the night of Double Seven (the seventh day of the Seventh Month, which is the first month of autumn in the traditional Chinese calendar), when magpies form a bridge for their sake. Throughout the centuries Double Seven has remained a popular festival that was especially celebrated by women, who prayed for skill in needlework on this night.

Later accounts tried to explain why these lovers were separated. According to the sixth-century *Annual Customs of Jing and Chu* (*Jing Chu suishi ji*) by Zong Lin (c. 500–c. 563), Buffalo Boy had failed to pay back the money he had borrowed for the wedding gifts:

---

[1]   Quoted in Yuan and Zhou, 1985, 113.

81

I once read in some Daoist book that Buffalo Boy, when marrying
Weaving Maiden, borrowed money from the God of Heaven for the
engagement gifts—when he had not repaid the money even after quite
some time he was banished to (the constellation) Barracks Room.[2]

The more common explanation in later centuries has been that the two
newlyweds indulged in marital delights to such an extent that they neglected the
chores implied by their names, and that as a punishment they were positioned
on opposite sides of the Heavenly River. The sixteenth-century *Extended Meanings
of the Monthly Ordinances* (*Yueling Guangyi*), quotes in its chapter on the Seventh
Month the following account:

> Weaving Maiden is positioned to the east of the Heavenly River; she is
> a child of the God of Heaven. Each and every year she labors and slaves
> at loom and shuttle, weaving colored brocade and heavenly garments.
> The God of Heaven pitied her for her lonely life, and promised her in
> marriage to Buffalo Boy on the western side of the River. Following the
> wedding she thereupon neglected her weaving and sewing. In his anger
> the God of Heaven punished her by ordering her to go back to the
> eastern side of the River. Only in the night of the seventh day of the
> Seventh Month she crosses the River for a meeting.[3]

The Extended Meanings of the Monthly Ordinances mentions as its source *xiaoshuo*, which
could be a reference to the sixth-century *Minor Tales* (*Xiaoshuo*), a collection of
anecdotes by a certain Yin Yun, but could also refer to the sixteenth-century
novel (*xiaoshuo*) on the legend of Weaving Maiden and Buffalo Boy.

The innumerable references to this myth in later poetry, prose, drama, and
fiction hardly, if ever, go beyond the simple details of these classical accounts.
Modern surveys of classical Chinese mythology, therefore, often flesh out
these meager accounts with the contents of modern folktales,[4] rather than
incorporating a classical tale of the Tang dynasty that has Weaving Maiden
cheat on Buffalo Boy with a handsome mortal lover.[5] A full translation of this

---

[2]   Quoted in Hong Shuling, 1988, 45. This passage is not included in current editions of Zong
Lin's work, but it is quoted in the eighteenth-century *Peiwen Compendium of Rhymes* (*Peiwen yunfu*). A
comparable story is quoted, however, in *The Imperial Readings of the Taiping Era* (*Taiping yulan*) of the late
tenth century.

[3]   Quoted in Yuan and Zhou, 1985, 113. *The Peiwen Compendium of Rhymes* quotes the same passage and
credits it to *Annual Customs of Jing and Chu*. See Hong Shuling, 1988, 45.

[4]   Birrell, 1993, 165–7; Yang and An, 2005, 221; Yuan, 1993, 183–6.

[5]   Li Fang, 1961, 420–1, "Guo Han." The text derives from *Mysterious Miracles* (*Lingguai ji*) by Zhang

tale by Zhang Jian (744–804), entitled *Guo Han* after the Weaving Maiden's love interest, is presented here.[6] Roughly eight hundred years later, a sixteenth-century author called Zhu Mingshi devoted a short novel to Weaving Maiden and Buffalo Boy entitled *The Tale of Buffalo Boy and Weaving Maiden (Niulang Zhinü zhuan)*, but his work survived only in a single copy and has been universally ignored. In the early years of the twentieth century there appeared yet another short novel on the same theme and with the same title that did not fare much better. The summaries of these two novels that follow the translation of *Guo Han* have been translated from the entries by Shu Mu in *Zhongguo gudai xiaoshuo zongmu*, edited by Shi Changyu (Taiyuan: Shanxi Jiaoyu Chubanshe, 2004), Vol. 2, *Baihua juan*, 241–42.[7]

Zhang Jian, *Guo Han*

In his youth Guo Han from Taiyuan despised those in power and distinguished himself by his purity. He struck a handsome figure, knew his way with words, and was an expert in cursive script and the clerical style. From early on he had been an orphan and he lived all by himself. Once, in the heat of the summer, he had made his bed in the courtyard by the light of the moon. Suddenly there was a clear breeze, and he smelled a faint fragrance that became increasingly stronger. He was very much perplexed by this, and when he looked up into the sky, someone, he saw, was slowly descending to earth. Upon arrival she turned out to be a young girl. Her brilliant beauty was not of this world, and her resplendent luster dazzled your eyes! She wore a gown of black silk and trailed a stole of frostlike gauze. On her head she wore a cap of tall kingfisher feathers adorned with phoenix couples, and her feet were shod in sandals decorated with jasper in multiple patterns. Her two servant girls were both exceptionally beautiful, unsettling your heart and soul!

Han straightened his gown and head scarf, stepped down from his couch, and addressed her with a bow: "Please be so kind as to speak to me, oh noble divinity, now that you have so unexpectedly descended from on high!" Smiling, she answered: "I am Weaving Maiden from heaven up above. Because I have been without a partner for so long, and the annual reunion is nowhere in sight, I was overcome by melancholy, so the Emperor on High kindly told me to

---

Jian (774–804). On Zhang Jian and his *Mysterious Miracles*, see Li Jianguo, 1993, 456–63.

[6]   The translation is based on Wang Rutao, 1980, 478–85.

[7]   For a convenient compendium of major Chinese articles on various aspects of the legend of Buffalo Boy and Weaving Maiden, see Tao, 2006.

visit the world of mortals. Out of admiration for your pure style, I would like to entrust myself to your friendship." Han replied: "This is beyond my wildest expectations. Now I'm moved even deeper!" Weaving Maiden thereupon ordered her maids to clean and sweep the room and to affix bed curtains of red crepe like a frosty mist. When they spread out a mat of water crystal and flowery jade and moved their breeze-assembling fans, it was just as cool as in pure autumn. Hand in hand they then stepped inside and, loosening their gowns, they lay down together. The pink raw-silk shift that touched her skin resembled a little fragrance pouch, and its perfume filled the whole room. Their heads rested on a united-hearts headrest made of camphor wood, and they slept under a double-thread coverlet with a pattern of mandarin ducks. Her soft skin and tender body, her deep love and secret gestures manifested voluptuousness without precedent! When the sky was about to break and she took her leave, her powdered face was just as it had been the night before, but when he tried to wipe her face, this turned out to be her natural looks. Han accompanied her into the garden, and then she left, rising through the clouds.

From that moment on, she came every night, and their love and affection only became more intense. Han teased her by asking: "Where is Buffalo Boy? How do you dare go out by yourself?" She answered him: "The transformations of yin and yang are none of his business. Moreover, he has no way of knowing because we are separated by the Heavenly River. And even if he would come to know about us, there's no need for you to worry." Stroking Han's breast, she then said: "It's all because people of this world cannot see things clearly!" Han continued by asking: "Could you tell me something about the celestial images as you yourself have entrusted your soul to such a celestial image?" She answered him: "When people in this world observe them, they only see them as stars, but in that realm there are palaces and houses, where the immortals roam. The essences of the ten thousand beings and things all have their image in the sky and take shape here on earth. The developments in the world of man are all manifested up above. When I observe the sky, everything is perfectly clear to me." She thereupon pointed the locations of the constellations out to Han and detailed their degrees and grades, and as a result Han came to know everything that ordinary people did not know.

Later, when Double Seven was approaching, she suddenly did not come anymore, and she only showed up again after quite some nights. Han asked her: "Was it a pleasant meeting?" Smiling, she answered him: "How could heaven above ever compare with the world here below! I had to do it because of fate, and for no other reason, so don't be jealous!" When he asked her: "How come it took you so much time?" she replied: "Five days in the world of man are one night over there." She also procured Han some heavenly dishes, and none of them was made of worldly foods. When he closely observed her gown, it had no stitches, and when he asked her about it, she told him: "Heavenly gowns are not put together with needle and thread." Whenever she left, she made sure to take all her clothes with her.

After a full year, suddenly one evening she looked miserable. As her tears coursed down, she grasped Han's hands and said: "The order of the Emperor on High has reached its term, so we have to say good-bye forever." And she sobbed uncontrollably. When a startled and alarmed Han asked her: "How many days have we left?" she replied: "Only tonight!" Thereupon they wept piteously and didn't sleep all night. When daybreak arrived, they held each other tightly as they parted. She gave him a seven-jewel bowl as a keepsake and told him that she would send him a letter next year on such and such a day. In his turn Han gave her a pair of jade bracelets. She then disappeared, walking through the air; looking back, she waved at him, and only after quite a while did she disappear.

The next year at the appointed time she indeed had her servant girls of before deliver a letter to Han. When he opened the envelope, she had used blue silk as paper and written the characters using cinnabar. Her words were pure and refined, and her love and attachment had only increased. At the end of the letter there were two poems, the first of which read:

> The Heavenly River may be wide so wide;
> There still is that early autumn rendezvous.
> But for my lover it's finished now for ever—
> When will we ever be able to meet again?

The second poem read:

> Red towers look down on a pure river;
> Jasper palaces connect to purple rooms.
> The desire for a reunion still is there,
> But it is only good to break my heart.

Han wrote her a letter in reply on a piece of scented paper, which gave expression to his desperation. He also wrote two quatrains, the first of which went:

> Since ancient times the world of man
> Cannot set its hopes on heaven above.
> Who knew that by once looking back
> Both of us would be filled by longing?

His second poem read:

The headrest you gave to me still is fragrant;
My gown still shows the traces of your tears.
Your face is displayed at the celestial river—
All in vain, our souls try to go back and forth.

From that moment on they had no further contact.

That year the Grand Astronomer reported to the throne that the Weaving Maiden Star lacked luster.

Han continued to long for her, and even the most gorgeous women in the world of man could not attract his attention. But because he needed an heir, it was decided that he needed to marry, and so against his own wishes he took a daughter of the Cheng family as his wife. She did not please him at all, and they became bitter enemies, also because the marriage remained childless.

Eventually Han passed away after reaching the rank of attendant censor.

Summaries of Novels

Zhu Mingshi, *The Tale of Buffalo Boy and Weaving Maiden* (*Niulang Zhinü zhuan*), in Four Parts (*juan*) (fifty-five sections)

This is a novel of the Wanli period (1573–1619) of the Ming dynasty. The author is the "Confucian student Zhu Mingshi (Taiti)," but no details are known about his life. The novel has been preserved in a printing by Yu Chengzhang from Xianyuan. Because Yu Chengzhang was a nephew of Yu Xiangdou, a publisher from Jiangyang in Fujian during the Wanli period, the novel must have been printed during the Wanli period.

The novel tells the story of Buffalo Boy and Weaving Maiden. Buffalo Boy lives on the western side of the Heavenly River, and Weaving Maiden lives on the eastern side of the Heavenly River. Year after year Weaving Maiden labors at the loom, weaving heavenly garments of cloud brocade. The Jade Emperor pities her for her hard work and loneliness and allows her to marry Buffalo Boy from the other side of the river. Once Weaving Maiden and Buffalo Boy have been married, they do not work as hard at their tasks of plowing and weaving as they used to do, because they are so much in love with each other as husband and wife. The Jade Emperor is enraged and banishes Weaving Maiden to the western side of the river. Only because of a later petition by the immortals are the lovers allowed to come together once each year. A poem at the beginning of the first part reads:

Weaving Maiden at the Heavenly River was most skilled;
The Jade Emperor gave her in marriage to Buffalo Boy.
Man and wife indulged in lust and neglected their duties,
So they were banished to the clouds both east and west.
   Following a petition, they meet once on Double Seven;
Magpies then construct a bridge for them on their behalf.
Men and women together pray to her for the gift of skill,
As her fine reputation permeates into the inner quarters.

This summarizes the plot of this novel.

   This book has been written on the basis of folk legend. The *Yueling guangyi* by
Feng Yingjing of the Ming dynasty records this story in *juan* 14 and states that
it derives from *Xiaoshuo*, but neither Yin Yun's *Xiaoshuo* nor Liu Song's *Xiaoshuo*
contains the story of Buffalo Boy and Weaving Maiden, so it is unclear to
which work this title may refer.

Anonymous, *The Tale of Buffalo Boy and Weaving Maiden* (*Niulang Zhinü zhuan*), in Twelve Chapters (c.1910)

This work is not divided into *juan*; it is made up of twelve chapters. It is a novel
from the end of the Qing; no author is mentioned.

   Weaving Maiden is a grandchild of the Jade Emperor, the Seventh Immortal
Maiden of the Bushel and Buffalo Palace. The Golden Lad is a page serving the
Jade Emperor. One day, when he is ordered to borrow the warm-and-hot jade
cups of the Sagely Mother, it just so happens that the Sagely Mother is not at
home. By chance he meets with Weaving Maiden, and the two of them fall in
love at first sight. The Sagely Mother is very unhappy about this and reports the
matter to the Jade Emperor. As punishment, the latter orders Weaving Maiden
to go and weave brocade in the Cloud Brocade Palace on the eastern bank of
the Heavenly River, and he banishes the Golden Lad to the mortal world here
below to experience suffering. The Golden Lad is born in the Niu (Buffalo)
family of Luoyang. Upon the death of his parents, he suffers all kinds of
mistreatment at the hands of his sister-in-law, so he spends all his days with
the plowing buffalo.

   After thirteen years the Sagely Mother is filled with sympathy for his plight,
and in a letter to the Jade Emperor she asks him to show some sympathy.
The Jade Emperor dispatches an immortal to enlighten Buffalo Boy, and he
also allows Buffalo Boy and Weaving Maiden to get married and live in the

Numinous Splendor Palace on the western side of the Heavenly River. But once the two of them are married, they spend all day in their own little world and don't even go and pay their respect to the Sagely Mother. The Sagely Mother once again reports them to the Jade Emperor, who in a fit of rage orders Weaving Maiden for all eternity to weave brocade in the Cloud Brocade Palace on the eastern side of the Heavenly River.

Buffalo Boy and Weaving Maiden now are separated by the Heavenly River and cannot meet, so both of them are filled with anger and resentment. The Metal Star of Great White (the planet Venus) and the Old Lord of Great Supremity (Laozi) submit a report to the throne in which they ask for pity, whereupon the Jade Emperor allows the couple to meet once each year on the seventh day of the Seventh Month.

The contents of this novel are quite different from *The Tale of Buffalo Boy and Weaving Maiden* in four *juan* that was printed in the Ming dynasty, because the latter does not include the fact that Buffalo Boy and Weaving Maiden fall in love at first sight and all the later developments that are caused by their falling in love at first sight. The only place in which this novel continues the Ming-dynasty novel is in the incidents of Buffalo Boy and Weaving Maiden indulging in the pleasures of marital life, thereby causing the Jade Emperor to become enraged, ordering them to opposite sides of the Heavenly River. This book must have been written on the basis of folk legends, and it is not a rewriting of *The Tale of Buffalo Boy and Weaving Maiden* in four *juan* of the Ming. (Also see the entry on *The Tale of Buffalo Boy and Weaving Maiden* in four *juan*.)

This novel has been preserved in a lithographic edition from the Daguan Shuju in Shanghai of c. 1910. . . . There is also a 1937 typeset edition from the Minzhong Shudian in Shanghai. The text has been reprinted by Lu Gong in his *Guben pinghua xiaoshuo ji* (Renmin Wenxue Chubanshe, 1984) on the basis of the lithographic edition of the Daguan Shuju in Shanghai.[8]

---

[8]   Lu Gong makes the erroneous claim that the late-Qing novel is a rewriting of the Ming novel.

II

MODERN FOLKTALES &
REGIONAL PLAYS

Once Chinese scholars in the 1920s and 1930s started to collect oral literature, fairy tales about Weaving Maiden and Buffalo Boy were recorded all over China. The selection presented here is taken from Hong Shuling, *Niulang Zhinü yanjiu* (Taipei: Xuesheng Shuju, 1988), pp. 152–61. Hong Shuling has collected many versions and distinguishes three types of stories: (1) the two brothers; (2) the banished immortals; and (3) the fighting couple. The stories of the first type are by far the most common. Each of these types is here represented by two or more examples.[9]

Stories of the first type also have been adapted for the stage in various genres of traditional regional theater. Here we only present a summary of an adaptation of a Yuju (Henan opera) play entitled *Heavenly River Match*. The summary has been translated from Ma Zichen, Ed., *Zhongguo Yuju dacidian* (Zhengzhou: Zhongzhou Guji Chubanshe, 1998), p. 463.

Buffalo Boy and Weaving Maiden (Fengtian)

Wang Little Two is living with his elder brother and wife. Because he is alerted by the brown buffalo, he escapes being murdered by poison. Later the elder brother and the younger brother divide the inheritance, and the only thing Wang Little Two gets is the brown buffalo.

The brown buffalo suddenly changes into an old man who says that he is actually a banished star, and that after his death gourd sprouts will grow from his grave, and that Little Two will find happiness if he goes off in the direction indicated by the sprouts. When Wang Little Two follows his advice and sets out, he indeed finds a beautiful girl who is taking a bath in the river. When he then runs off with her clothes, she agrees to become his wife. She also tells him that she is the daughter of the Queen Mother of the West and is called Weaving Maiden.

Later, Weaving Maiden and Wang Little Two ascended to heaven to offer their congratulations to the Queen Mother on the occasion of her birthday.

---

[9] Hong Shuling has also collected numerous stories that link the origin of customs and place-names to the legend of the Weaving Maiden and the Cowherd, but such stories are not included in this small selection.

The Queen Mother berates the two of them and separates them by drawing a river with one of her golden hairpins, and she orders that they can only see each other on the seventh day of the Seventh Month of each year.

Collected and recorded by Hong Zhenzhou.

Buffalo Boy and Weaving Maiden (Yongjia in Zhejiang)

Buffalo Boy, a young kid who was looking after the buffalo, one day was alerted by the brown buffalo and so could escape from the vicious plot of his elder brother and his wife. He then asked his uncle to take charge of the division of their inheritance. Buffalo Boy insisted that he only wanted the old brown buffalo, the broken cart, and the broken leather chest.

The old brown buffalo was actually a banished immortal from heaven and also taught him a method to obtain a beautiful wife. Buffalo Boy set off according to his instructions, and indeed in the river there was a girl who was just taking a bath. Buffalo Boy grabbed her clothes, and Weaving Maiden then became his wife, and after three years, she had given him two children.

One day the brown buffalo informed him that it would go back to heaven and told him that if he would wear boots made of its leather, he could pursue his fleeing wife. Weaving Maiden indeed secretly got access to the clothes she had been wearing when taking a bath a long time ago and rose up into the sky. Buffalo Boy put on his leather boots and pursued her with the children. Weaving Maiden pulled out one of her golden hairpins and drew a heavenly river to block Buffalo Boy. Now the two of them stood each on one side of this river and kept on throwing the buffalo's yoke and the weaving shuttle at each other.

The God of Heaven showed up in person to effect a peace, but the quail mistakenly turned his order "See each other every seventh" into "See each other on the seventh of the Seventh." To this very day the quail still is calling "Not right! Not right!" hoping to correct his mistake.

Collected and recorded by Zheng Shichao.

The Story of the Banks of the Heavenly River (Guanyun in Jiangsu)

Once upon a time there lived a poor young man whose only possession was an old water buffalo, so the people called him Buffalo Boy. The old buffalo told him: "Seven immortal maidens are taking a bath in the river, and if you steal the precious garment of one of them, you can make that one your wife." Buffalo Boy indeed obtained a wife in this manner, and her name was River Weaving Maiden (He Zhinü).

Not long after this the old buffalo died of some disease, and it told Buffalo Boy to fill its skin with sand and bind it up as a sack with the rope through its nose, because later that would be of use to him.

A few years later, when Weaving Maiden had given birth to one boy and one girl, she tricked Buffalo Boy with sweet words into giving back her precious garment and then rode off on a cloud. Accompanied by his children, Buffalo Boy set out in pursuit with the buffalo-hide sack of sand on his back. Weaving Maiden drew a river with a golden hairpin, but Buffalo Boy emptied the sack of sand into the river, and so a sandbank appeared in the river. Weaving Maiden then drew a heavenly river, but Buffalo Boy was out of sand to fill it up. Thereupon he threw the rope through the nose of the buffalo to the other side, and Weaving Maiden countered that by throwing her shuttle. These are the modern Buffalo Rope Star and the Shuttle Star.

The God of Heaven showed up in person to bring about a reconciliation and ordered each of them to live on one side of the river and to meet one time each year on the seventh of the Seventh Month on the eastern side of the river.

Collected and recorded by Sun Jiaxun.

Buffalo Boy (Shandong)

The elder brother of Buffalo Boy had left home to make money, and he was always ill-treated by his sister-in-law. But because he was alerted by the old buffalo, he did not eat the poisoned dumpling by which she tried to murder him. So he invited his uncle to divide the inheritance and got the old buffalo and a broken cart.

Just before dying, the old buffalo told him that he should wrap himself in the buffalo's skin and then, when he got to the Heavenly River, he would find nine girls taking a bath in the river. Buffalo Boy set out as he was told, and indeed managed to steal one of the immortal garments, and so married one of the immortal maidens.

A few years later, the immortal maiden had given birth to one boy and one girl. By a deceptive trick she got her heavenly garment back, and once she had put it on, she rose into the sky and disappeared. With his children in his arms Buffalo Boy set off in pursuit. Her Majesty the Queen Mother who was just cooking rice heard the immortal maiden cry for help, and so she kept Buffalo Boy out by the method of drawing water to make a river.

The immortal maiden said to the Queen Mother that she wanted to spend most of the days at her mother's place, and so Her Majesty the Queen Mother ordered the two of them to be together from the first day of the Seventh Month to the seventh day of the Seventh Month of each year. From that time on, magpies build a bridge for them on the first day of the Seventh Month of each year, and on the seventh day, the two of them say good-bye, crying profusely.

Told by Zhao Shuwen.

Sun Shouyi and the Fifth Immortal Maiden (Hebei)

Sun Shouyi from Zhili was living with his elder brother and his wife. His elder brother loved him dearly, but he was regularly away from home for trade. His sister-in-law used every opportunity to maltreat him—she doted on her own father and despised her brother-in-law. Alerted by the brown buffalo, Sun Shouyi did not eat the poisoned food by which she wanted to murder him. He invited his uncle to divide the inheritance, and all he got was the brown buffalo.

The old brown buffalo told him that it was the Golden Buffalo Star who had come down to earth and ordered Shouyi to go to the pond on the eastern side—there he would find nine immortal maidens taking a bath, and he should take the fifth set of clothes. Shouyi set out as directed and indeed got the Fifth Immortal Maiden as his wife.

A few years later she had given birth to one boy and one girl. Just before his death the old brown buffalo told Shouyi to keep the buffalo head, because if he raised it, he could fly to heaven. The Queen Mother dispatched heavenly troops to bring Weaving Maiden back to the heavenly palace. Shouyi, carrying the children on his back, promptly set off in pursuit: by lifting the buffalo head, he rose up to heaven.

When the Queen Mother saw this situation, she took down a golden hairpin and drew the Heavenly River to block Shouyi's way. Shouyi and his children wept continuously for three days and three nights, and only then did Her Majesty the Queen Mother allow Shouyi and his wife to meet on the seventh day of the Seventh Month, ordering a hundred birds to build the magpie bridge.

Collected and recorded by Wang Qiang.

The Veterinarian Niu Lang (Buffalo Boy) (Yunan)

On the banks of the Huai lived the son of an old buffalo veterinarian who was called Niu Lang. Because Niu Lang had treated and cured one thousand buffalo, Guanyin promoted him to the rank of the immortals.[10] At just that moment Weaving Maiden, the youngest daughter of Her Majesty the Queen

---

[10] The bodhisattva Guanyin has been one of the most widely revered Chinese deities ever since she was introduced into China in the fourth century. Initially Guanyin was venerated in the guise of a handsome prince, but from the tenth century on, the bodhisattva was often venerated in female guise.

Mother, showed her face from the side, which ruined his chance of becoming an immortal, so Niu Lang returned to the world of men. Weaving Maiden promptly followed him to this mortal world and became his wife. The next year she gave birth to twins. The boy was called Niu Xiaolang (Buffalo Little Boy) and the girl was called Niu Zhinü (Buffalo Weaving Maiden).

On the seventh day of the Seventh Month the Jade Emperor dispatched heavenly soldiers to arrest Weaving Maiden. In her panic she left behind only one pair of slippers. Niu Lang put on her slippers, held his children by the hand, and preceded by magpies who showed him the way, flew up to heaven. When he had almost caught up with her, the Jade Emperor employed the magic method for immobilizing a body, so Niu Lang was immobilized on that spot, and the Jade Emperor ordered the heavenly soldiers to give him a beating.

Her Majesty the Queen Mother could not bear this, and she also was afraid that Niu Lang might still want to steal Weaving Maiden, so she took out a golden hairpin and drew the Heavenly River to block Niu Lang. Niu Lang and his children cried and cried without end, so Her Majesty the Queen Mother then asked the Jade Emperor to show pity, but he only allowed them to see each other on this very day, but he did not build a bridge for them. The magpies offered themselves as volunteers to build them a bridge.

If you now lift your head and look at the sky, the two little stars on both sides of Buffalo Boy are Niu Xiaolang and Niu Zhinü, and all the other big and small stars are their tears. Each year on the seventh day of the Seventh Month all magpies fly to heaven to build a bridge. And if one lies down in a pepper field or under a grape arbor, one can still hear the weeping of Buffalo Boy and Weaving Maiden.

Collected and recorded by Yang Zhuze.

Buffalo Boy and Weaving Maiden (Southern Fujian)

Buffalo Boy was a poor boy, and Weaving Maiden was a rich girl. Weaving Maiden had sworn an oath that she would marry any man who could make her laugh. One day she was combing her seven-foot two-inch long hair using a hair rack.[11] When the bald-headed Buffalo Boy imitated her, he caused her to smile. Weaving Maiden told her servant Yuehen to tell Buffalo Boy that he should come and have a rendezvous with her. When Weaving Maiden did not see Buffalo Boy, she fell sick for longing and died. Buffalo Boy sacrificed at her grave and, once home, also fell ill and died.

---

[11] From the context it would appear that a "hair rack" was a wooden contraption on which to spread out one's long hair for quick drying or easy combing.

The two of them originally had been stars in heaven, and upon their death they both reassumed their immortal rank, but they still meet only once, on the seventh of the Seventh Month. Buffalo Boy brings along the three hundred and sixty bowls he has accumulated [over the year], and gives them to Weaving Maiden so she can clean them. But when she is done cleaning, the time for their separation has already arrived. This is why Weaving Maiden greatly hates the magpie for messing up, and she pulls out the feathers on the head of the magpie, and so the magpies all get bald on the Seventh Night.

Narrated by Cai Weixiao.

Buffalo Boy and Weaving Maiden (Southern Fujian)

Buffalo Boy and Weaving Maiden, these two divine stars, had committed an offense against the heavenly regulations at the birthday banquet of the Queen Mother, and they were banished to the world of men. Weaving Maiden was born as the daughter of a rich family, and Buffalo Boy was born as the son of a poor family.

One day, when Weaving Maiden was trying to get some relief from the heat, her [bare] arm was seen by Buffalo Boy, so she made up her mind that he would be her husband. She thereupon dispatched her servant Chuntao with a message. But when her father learned of this, he had Weaving Maiden locked up, so Buffalo Boy went home, all disappointed. Weaving Maiden then ordered the magpie to transmit a message, but the magpie made the mistake of saying "meet me on the seventh day of the Seventh Month" instead of "meet me every day that has a seven." Buffalo Boy then fell ill for love-longing and died, and Weaving Maiden committed suicide.

When the two of them had gone to heaven following their death, they beseeched the Jade Emperor to be reborn again, but he did not give his permission. But he did give them permission to see each other once every year on the Seventh Night, when magpies build a bridge.

Narrated by Ouyang Feiyun.

The Tale of the Seventh Night (Chaozhou)

Buffalo Boy and Weaving Maiden were originally immortals, but because their carnal desires were somewhat aroused when they met with each other in the clouds, they were banished to the red dust by the Jade Emperor. They were born in families related through marriage, and they were married once they had grown up. At the behest of his father, Buffalo Boy was living away from home for business, while Weaving Maiden stayed at home, weaving cloth. When

Buffalo Boy's father was critically ill, his final instructions were: "Make sure that you come home once on every day with a seven." But the old servant made a mistake and told him that he should come home once, on the seventh day of the Seventh Month. Buffalo Boy, being a very filial son, strictly followed that instruction, not daring to disobey.

Now that the two of them have died and returned to the world of the immortals, they still only meet once every year, on the seventh day of the Seventh Month. If you look at the stars in heaven, the two little stars in front of Weaving Maiden are the infants she is still nursing, so she has to carry them at her breast. The two stars on both sides of Buffalo Boy are their grown-up sons, who follow their father. For their rendezvous on Seventh Night, Buffalo Boy borrows a shuttle-shaped star as his boat to cross the Heavenly River.

Narrated by Cheng Yunxiang.

The Story of Buffalo Boy and Weaving Maiden of Mrs. Wang

Buffalo Boy was called Shanbo, and Weaving Maiden was called Yingtai. The two of them fell in love when they studied together, but eventually they failed to become a couple. Shanbo died for love, and Yingtai committed suicide by jumping into his grave. The servant of the Ma family (to whom Yingtai had been engaged by her parents) threw the two rocks in the coffins on the two sides of a river, but from these rocks grew two trees with intertwining branches. The servants of the Ma family then put a torch to these trees, and in the flames the trees rose up to heaven, where they became the Buffalo Boy Star and the Weaving Maiden Star, placed to the east and the west of the Silver River.

When Buffalo Boy and Weaving Maiden had ascended to heaven, the Jade Emperor discovered that they had a karmic bond as husband and wife, and so he permitted the two of them to meet once a year for seven days and seven nights. Who could have known that the two of them did not hear him clearly, so they believed that they could meet only once a year on the night of the seventh day of the Seventh Month. Since then, there always falls a light rain on the night of the seventh day of the Seventh Month, and that rain is the tears of these lovers.

Narrated by Wang Fuqiao.

Liu Niulang and Zhou Zhinü (Hubei)

Liu Niulang (Buffalo Boy) had come at the age of eight to the house of the Zhous to herd their buffalo. The only child of the Zhous, a daughter, was good at weaving brocades. On Double Fifth one year Zhinü had gone out to watch the dragon boats. Because she tried to avoid some evil people who were trying to take advantage of her, she stumbled and fell into a pond, but fortunately she was saved by Niulang. She was deeply moved in her heart and gave him clothes and shoes. The two of them fell deeply in love with each other. When Mr. Zhou learned about this, he flew into a rage. That very night Niulang and Zhinü ran away from the Zhou mansion, and when they arrived at some other place, they married each other and had one son and one daughter.

Later Zhinü was found and brought back by her father's servants, and Mr. Zhou only agreed after piteous prayers that the two of them could see each other each year on the seventh day of the Seventh Month.

Collected and recorded by Tao Jian.

How Buffalo Boy and Weaving Maiden Became Sworn Enemies (Hebei)

Weaving Maiden, the youngest daughter of Her Majesty the Queen Mother, secretly descended to the mortal world to become the wife of Buffalo Boy. Her Majesty the Queen Mother had her fetched home, and Buffalo Boy followed her to the heavenly palace. But because he was not used to palace life, he always was fighting with Weaving Maiden.

On the seventh day of the Seventh Month one year, the two of them were again having a fight. Buffalo Boy threw his buffalo bow at Weaving Maiden, and she countered with her shuttle. Right at that very moment Her Majesty the Queen Mother passed by, and as she was not used to them fighting, she took down a hairpin and drew the Heavenly River to separate the two of them. She only allowed them to meet on the seventh day of the Seventh Month of each year.

Nowadays the three little stars by the side of the Weaving Maiden Star are the buffalo bow, and the three shuttle-shaped stars by the side of the Buffalo Boy Star are Weaving Maiden's shuttle.

Narrated by Dong Zhanshun.

How Weaving Maiden Changed Her Mind (Subei)

Weaving Maiden was a granddaughter of the Jade Emperor. She was called the Heaven's Grandchild Star and worked hard at weaving. Buffalo Boy was a common guy who worked the land here on earth. One day he had crossed the river to cut grass, and inadvertently he had taken the flowers Weaving Maiden was weaving into her cloud brocade for true flowers and cut them down. So he could only make it up to Weaving Maiden, and since that time he had won her love.

Weaving Maiden asked Her Majesty the Queen Mother to agree to their marriage, but the Queen Mother refused to do so. The Golden Buffalo Star, who always had been a good friend of Buffalo Boy, then discussed the matter with the Southern Pole Immortal Greybeard, but even when the latter and Guanyin played the matchmaker, they did not succeed.[12] The Golden Buffalo Star then carried Weaving Maiden on his back and descended to the mortal world so the two of them could be married. He himself also turned into an old buffalo to work for Buffalo Boy. Later Weaving Maiden gave birth to a boy and a girl.

But as time went by, Buffalo Boy grew ever more dark and gaunt, while Weaving Maiden remained beautiful and white as before, and she started to have remorse. All day long she was lazy and indolent, and she became a typical lazy wife. So when one day the Kui Tree Wolf descended to earth to urge her to return to heaven, she followed him. The Golden Buffalo Star then changed himself into a buffalo skin, two buffalo horns, and two buffalo ears, and nine ribs, which he handed to Buffalo Boy, and he told him to ascend to heaven in pursuit, carrying his children before his breast and on his back in the two baskets of his carrying pole.

When he arrived at the Southern Gate of Heaven, Buffalo Boy scared the Hound of Heaven off with his buffalo horns. And when the Kui Tree Wolf threw down the Queen Mother's jade bowl, which then changed into a huge ocean, Buffalo Boy covered it with the buffalo skin, whereupon it turned into a carpet of grass on which he could walk easily. Even though Weaving Maiden could not bear to hear her children cry, she still clenched her teeth and went on forward. When she saw that Buffalo Boy was catching up with her, she pulled out a golden hairpin and drew three lines on the ground, which turned into nine rivers of gold. Buffalo Boy scooped nine handfuls of earth from the buffalo ears and in that way filled up each of them. Weaving Maiden then pulled out a silver hairpin and drew nine silver rivers one after another. At first Buffalo Boy threw two ribs to fill a river, but later he threw one rib each time, so when he came to the ninth river, he was unable to fill it up. Buffalo Boy and Weaving Maiden now were stuck each on one side of the river. In order to vent their spite, the two of them threw the buffalo rope and the shuttle at each other.

Because Weaving Maiden longed for her children, she asked the Jade Emperor for help, but he only allowed her to meet them once on the seventh day of the Seventh Month. The Golden Buffalo Star then asked the magpies of the whole world to build them a bridge. That's why nowadays buffalo and magpies get along so well. Buffalo Boy and Weaving Maiden throwing things at each other across the river is the beginning of couples in this world throwing things and smashing furniture. The three stars in the bosom of the Weaving Maiden

---

[12] The Southern Pole Immortal Greybeard is a popular deity in charge of longevity.

Star are the buffalo rope that Buffalo Boy threw at her, and they are called the buffalo-rope stars. The four stars to the northeast of the Buffalo Boy Star are the shuttle that she threw at him, and they are called the shuttle stars. Buffalo Boy used two baskets on his carrying pole to carry the children, the boy in front and the girl on his back, and that is why sons are considered weighty and girls of little weight.

Collected and narrated by Ben Liu.

Heavenly River Match (*Tianhe pei*)

This play is also known as "Meeting at Magpie Bridge," "Uncle Divides the Inheritance," "The Seventh of the Seventh Month," and "Buffalo Boy and Weaving Maiden." It is a text that was transmitted orally by Chen Diansan. The plot goes back to a story in *Annual Customs of Jing and Chu (Jing Chu suishi ji)*.

The Sun family has practiced goodness for generations. The family has two sons—the elder being Shouren, the younger being Shouyi. Shouren marries a wife whose maiden name is Lu, and she wants to kill Shouyi so the whole family estate will be hers. The Jade Emperor orders the Golden Buffalo Star to change into a yellow buffalo, descend to earth, and assist Shouyi. The buffalo is sold to the Sun family. When Shouyi is herding the buffalo in the hills, the buffalo speaks to him in human language, informing him that his brother's wife wants to kill him. When he comes back home at noontime for his lunch, there is poison in his rice, and the buffalo signals to Shouyi not to eat the rice. When his brother's wife scolds and beats him, Shouyi invites his uncle to supervise the division of the inheritance. On the advice of the yellow buffalo, Shouyi only wants the yellow buffalo, a broken cart, and a damaged leather suitcase. Then he and the buffalo rise into the air and disappear.

When they arrive at a place deeply hidden in the mountains, the yellow buffalo miraculously produces a farm, and he makes a living by plowing and sowing. One day, when he is herding the buffalo by the side of a river, he espies an immortal maiden who is taking a bath. The yellow buffalo tells Shouyi to steal Weaving Maiden's garment, and thereupon the two of them become a couple as man and wife, and they have a boy and a girl.

One evening Weaving Maiden tells Buffalo Boy (Shouyi) that their karmic affinity has come to an end, and they will have to say good-bye to each other. Buffalo Boy's weeping is unable to detain her, and suppressing her tears, Weaving Maiden rises up in the air. Shouyi follows the instructions left to him by the yellow buffalo on its death and, on shoes made of buffalo hide, pursues her with the children. But they are stopped by the Queen Mother, who pulls a pin from her hair and draws the Heavenly River. In tears, husband and wife face each other, each on one side of the river. Li Changgeng arrives with an edict of the Emperor, allowing them to meet once each year on the seventh of the Seventh Month, when a hundred birds will all come together and form a magpie bridge.

BIBLIOGRAPHY

Works in Chinese

Du Yingtao 杜穎陶, comp. *Dong Yong Chenxiang heji* 董永沉香合集. Shanghai: Gudian Wenxue Chubanshe, 1957.

Guo Xun 郭勛, comp. *Yongxi yuefu* 雍熙樂府. Taipei: Xinan Shuju, 1981.

Hong Bian 洪楩, comp. *Qingping shantan huaben* 清平山堂話本. Edited by Tan Zhengbi 譚正璧. Shanghai: Gudian Wenxue Chubanshe, 1957.

Hong Shuling 洪淑苓. *Niulang Zhinü yanjiu* 牛郎織女研究. Taipei: Xuesheng Shuju, 1988.

Ji Yonggui 纪永贵. *Dong Yong yu xian chuanshuo yanjiu* 董永遇仙传说研究. Hefei: Anhui Daxue Chubanshe, 2006.

Lang Jing 郎净. *Dong Yong gushi de zhanyan jiqi wenhua jiegou* 董永故事的展演及其文化结构. Shanghai: Shanghai Guji Chubanshe, 2005.

Lang Jing 郎净. *Dong Yong chuanshuo* 董永传说. Beijing: Zhongguo Shehui Chubanshe, 2008.

Li Fang 李昉, ed. *Taiping guangji* 太平廣記. Beijing: Zhonghua Shuju, 1961.

Li Jianguo 李建國. *Tang Wudai zhiguai chuanqi xulu* 唐五代志怪傳奇敘錄. Tianjin: Nankai Daxue Chubanshe, 1993.

Li Jianye 李建业 and Dong Jinyan 董金艳, eds. *Dong Yong yu xiao wenhua* 董永与孝文化. Jinan: Qi Lu Shushe, 2003.

Lu Gong 路工, ed. *Guben pinghua xiaoshuo ji* 古本平话小说集. Beijing: Renmin Wenxue Chubanshe, 1984.

Ma Zichen 马紫晨, ed. *Zhongguo Yuju dacidian* 中国豫剧大词典. Zhengzhou: Zhongzhou Guji Chubanshe, 1998.

Niulang Zhinü zhuan, Qianlong Ma Zaixing qigu zhuan 牛郎織女傳 潛龍馬再興七姑傳, *Guben xiaoshuo jicheng* 古本小說集成, Vol. 115. Shanghai: Shanghai Guji Chubanshe, 1990.

Qi Biaojia 祁彪佳. *Yuanshan tang qupin jupin jiaolu* 遠山堂曲品劇品校錄. Edited by Huang Chang 黃裳. Shanghai: Shanghai Chubanshe, 1955.

Quhai zongmu tiyao 曲海總目提要. Beijing: Renmin Chubanshe, 1959.

Shi Changyu 石昌渝, ed. *Zhongguo gudai xiaoshuo zongmu* 中国古代小说总目.
    Taiyuan: Shanxi Jiaoyu Chubanshe, 2004.

Sima Qian 司馬遷. *Shiji* 史記. Beijing: Zhonghua Shuju, 1959.

Tao Wei 陶玮, comp. *Mingjia tan Niulang Zhinü* 名家谈牛郎织女.
    Beijing: Wenhua Yishu Chubanshe, 2006.

Wang Liqi 王利器, comp. *Lidai xiaohua ji* 历代笑话集. Shanghai: Gudian
    Wenxue Chubanshe, 1957.

Wang Rutao 王汝涛 et al., anns. *Taiping guangji xuan* 太平广记选.
    Jinan: Qi Lu Shushe, 1980.

Wu Chongshu 吴崇恕, ed. *Xiaogan wenhua yanjiu* 孝感文化研究. Beijing:
    Shehui Kexue Wenxian Chubanshe, 1999.

Xiang Chu 项楚, ed. *Dunhuang bianwen xuanzhu* 敦煌变文选注. Chengdu:
    Ba Shu Shushe, 1989.

Xie Baogeng 谢宝耿, comp. *Zhongguo xiaodao jinghua* 中国孝道精华. Shanghai:
    Shanghai Shehui Kexueyuan Chubanshe, 2000.

Yuan Ke 袁珂 and Zhou Ming 周明, comp. *Zhongguo shenhua ziliao suibian*
    中国神话资料萃编. Chengdu: Sichuansheng Shehui Kexueyuan
    Chubanshe, 1985.

Zhao Jingshen 赵景深. "Dong Yong maishen de yanbian" 董永卖身的演变.
    In *Duqu xiaoji* 讀曲小記, 61–68. Beijing: Zhonghua Shuju, 1959.

Zhao Youwen 趙幼文, ann. *Cao Zhi ji jiaozhu* 曹植集校注. Taipei: Mingwen
    Shuju, 1985.

Zhongguo quyi zhi. Hubei juan 中国曲艺志湖北卷. Beijing: Xinhua Chubanshe, 1992.

Zhongguo quyi zhi. Hunan juan 中国曲艺志湖南卷. Beijing: ISBN Zhongxin, 2000.

Works in Western Languages

Baller, F. W. *The Sacred Edict, with a Translation of the Colloquial Rendering.* Sixth
    Edition. Shanghai: China Inland Mission, 1924.

Birrell, Anne. *Chinese Mythology: An Introduction.* With a Foreword by Yuan K'o.
    Baltimore: The Johns Hopkins University Press, 1993.

Boltz, William G. *"Hsiao ching."* In *Early Chinese Texts: A Bibliographical Guide,* edited by Michael Lowe, 141–53. Berkeley: The Society for the Study of Early China/The Institute for East Asian Studies, University of California, 1993.

Chan, Alan K. L., and Sor-hoon Tan, eds. *Filial Piety in Chinese Thought and History.* London: Routledge-Curzon, 2004.

Chen, Ivan. *The Book of Filial Duty.* London: John Murray, 1908.

Chow, Tse-tsung. "The Anti-Confucian Movement in Early Republican China." In *The Confucian Persuasion,* edited by Arthur P. Wright, 288–312. Stanford: Stanford University Press, 1960.

Cole, Allan. *Mothers and Sons in Chinese Buddhism.* Stanford: Stanford University Press, 1998.

Dars, Jacques, trans. *Contes de la Montange Sereine.* Paris: Gallimard, 1987.

DeWoskin, Kenneth, and J. I. Crump Jr., trans. *In Search of the Supernatural: The Written Record.* Stanford: Stanford University Press, 1996.

Epstein, Maram. "Sons and Mothers: The Social Construction of Filial Piety in Late-Imperial China." In *Love, Hatred, and Other Passions: Questions and Themes on Emotions in Chinese Culture,* edited by Paolo Santangelo and Donatella Guida, 285–300. Leiden: Brill, 2006.

Hanan, Patrick. *The Chinese Short Story: Studies in Dating, Authorship and Composition.* Cambridge, MA: Harvard University Press, 1973.

Holm, David. "The Exemplar of Filial Piety and the End of the Ape-men: Dong Yong in Guangxi and Guizhou Ritual Performance." *T'oung Pao* 90 (2004): 32–64.

Idema, Wilt L. *Meng Jiangnü Brings Down the Great Wall: Ten Versions of a Chinese Legend.* Seattle: Washington University Press, 2008.

Ikels, Charlotte, ed. *Filial Piety: Practice and Discourse in Contemporary East Asia.* Stanford: Stanford University Press, 2004.

Jordan, David K. "Folk Filial Piety in Taiwan: *The Twenty-four Filial Exemplars.*" In *The Psycho-Cultural Dynamics of the Confucian Family: Past and Present,* edited by Walter H. Slote, 47–112. Seoul: International Cultural Society of Korea, 1986.

Knapp, Keith N. *Selfless Offspring: Filial Children and Social Order in Medieval China.* Honolulu: University of Hawai'i Press, 2005.

Koehn, Alfred. *Filial Devotion in China.* Peking: Lotus Court, 1943.

Lee, Haiyan. *Revolution of the Heart: A Genealogy of Love in China, 1900–1950.* Stanford: Stanford University Press, 2007.

Lévi, Jean. "Dong Yong, le fils pieux et le mythe formosan de l'origine des singes." *Journal Asiatique* 272 No. 1–2 (1984): 83–132.

Li Qiancheng. "Faces of the Weaving Maid and the Herdboy: Tensions, Reconciliations, and the Doubling Device in 'The Pearl Shirt Reencountered.'" *Monumenta Serica* 50 (2002): 337–54.

Lu Hsün. *Dawn Blossoms Plucked at Dusk.* Translated by Yang Hsien-yi and Gladys Yang. Peking: Foreign Languages Press, 1976.

Lu, Tina. *Accidental Incest, Filial Cannibalism and Other Peculiar Encounters in Late Imperial Chinese Literature.* Cambridge, MA: Harvard University Asia Center, 2008.

Makeham, John. "Ming-chiao in the Eastern Han: Filial Piety, Reputation, and Office." *Hanxue yanjiu* 8 No. 2 (1990): 79–109.

McDougall, Bonnie. *Mao Zedong's "Talks at the Yan'an Conference on Literature and Art"—A Translation of the 1943 Text with Commentary.* Ann Arbor: Center for Chinese Studies, University of Michigan, 1980.

Miller, Allen L. "The Swan-Maiden Revisited: The Religious Significance of 'Divine Wife' Folktales with Special Reference to Japan." *Asian Folklore Studies* 46 No. 1 (1987): 55–86.

Pa Chin. *Family.* Introduction by Olga Lang. Garden City, NY: Anchor Books, 1972.

Pa Chin. *The Family.* Translated by Sidney Shapiro. Peking: Foreign Languages Press, 1958.

Rosemont, Henry, Jr., and Roger T. Ames. *The Chinese Classic of Family Reverence: A Philosophical Translation of the* Xiaojing. Honolulu: University of Hawai'i Press, 2009.

Shang Wei. Rulin waishi *and Cultural Transformation in Late Imperial China.* Cambridge, MA: Harvard University Asia Center, 2003.

Shaw, Norman. *Chinese Forest Trees and Timber Supply.* London: T. Fisher Unwin, 1914.

Snow, Justine T. *The Spider's Web. Goddesses of Light and Loom: Examining the Evidence for the Indo-European Origin of Two Ancient Chinese Deities. Sino-Platonic Papers* 118 (June 2002).

Ting, Nai-tung. *A Type Index of Chinese Folktales in the Oral Tradition and Major Works of Non-Religious Classical Literature.* Helsinki: Suomlainen Tiedeakatemia, 1978.

Waley, Arthur. *Ballads and Stories from Tun-huang.* London: George Allen and Unwin, 1960.

Wu Hung. *The Wu Liang Shrine. The Ideology of Early Chinese Pictorial Art.* Stanford: Stanford University Press, 1989.

Yang, Lihui, and Deming An, with Jessica Anderson Turner. *Handbook of Chinese Mythology*. Oxford: Oxford University Press, 2005.

Yu, Eric Kwan-wai. "Of Marriage, Labor and the Small Peasant Family: A Morphological and Feminist Study of the Cowherd and Weaving Maid Folktales." *Comparative Literature and Culture* 3 (1998): 11–51.

Yuan Ke. *Dragons and Dynasties: An Introduction to Chinese Mythology*. Selected and translated by Kim Echlin and Nie Zhixiong. London: Penguin Books, 1993.

GLOSSARY OF CHINESE TERMS

Ba Jin 巴金
bianwen 變文

Cao Pi 曹丕
Cao Zhi 曹植
Chang'e 嫦娥
chuanqi 傳奇
Chuanqi huikao 傳奇匯考

dan 石
Dong Si 董祀
Dong Yong 董永
Dong Yong yu xian zhuan 董永遇仙傳
Dong Zhong 董仲
Dong Zhongshu 董仲舒

Ershisi xiao 二十四孝

Fayuan zhulin 法苑珠林
Fu Hua 傅華

Gan Bao 干寶
Gu Jueyu 顧覺宇
Guanyin 觀音
Guiguzi 鬼谷子
Guo Han 郭翰
Gushi shijiu shou 古詩十九首

huaben 話本
Huaiyin fenbie 槐陰分別
Huang 黃
Huang Wenyang 黃文暘

Jia 家
Jing Chu suishi ji 荊楚歲事記
juan 卷

li (pear) 梨
li (separation) 離
Liang Shanbo 梁山伯
Lingguai ji 靈怪集
Lingzhi pian 靈芝篇
Liu Bang 劉邦
Liu Xiang 劉向
Liushijia xiaoshuo 六十家小說
Lu Ban 魯班
Lü Dongbin 呂洞賓

Maishen ji 賣身記
Mao Zedong 毛澤東
Mulian 目連

niulang 牛郎
Niulang Zhinü zhuan 牛郎織女傳

Pang Juan 龐涓
Peiwen yunfu 佩文韻府

Qi Biaojia 祁彪佳
qianniu 牽牛
Qixiannü 七仙女
Quhai mu 曲海目
Quhai zongmu tiyao 曲海總目提要

Saijin 賽金
Sanggu 喪鼓

107

Sanyuantang 三元堂
Soushen ji 搜神集
Sun Bin 孫賓

Taiping yulan 太平御覽
Tiandi 天帝
Tianxian ji 天仙記
Tianxianpei 天仙配

Wang Wei 王維
wange 挽歌
Wenyuantang 文元堂

Xiang Yu 項羽
xiao 孝
Xiao jing 孝經
Xiaofu 笑府
Xiaogan 孝感
xiaoge 孝歌
xiaoshuo 小說
Xiaoshuo 小說
Xiaozi zhuan 孝子傳
*Xinjuan Nanbei shishang yuefu yadiao
   Wanqu hexuan* 新鐫南北時尚雅
   調萬曲合選
xiwen 戲文

Yan Fengying 嚴鳳英
Yan Junping 嚴君平
Yangguan 陽關
Yao 姚
yiding fenkai 一錠分開
yiding fenkai 一定分開
Yin Yun 殷芸
Yuanshantang qupin 遠山堂曲品
Yudi 玉帝
Yuefu kaolüe 樂府考略
Yueling guangyi 月令廣義
Yuju 豫劇

zaju 雜劇
zao zi 早子
zaozi 棗子
Zeng Cen 曾參
Zhang Jian 張薦
Zhao Hei 趙黑
zhengshu 正書
Zhijin ji 織錦記
Zhijuan ji 織絹記
zhinü 織女
Zhu Mingshi 朱名世
Zhu Yingtai 祝英台
zhuangyuan 狀元
Zong Lin 宗懍